Joe jumped, when, suddenly, the museum's lights all went out at once. The room was plunged into complete darkness.

Joe heard some loud, sharp sounds coming from the direction of the door.

"Power failure!" someone yelled.

"I'm glad I backed up my files," David said. "It's really dark in here, isn't it?"

Joe felt Wishbone press against his leg. He reached down and patted the Jack Russell terrier reassuringly. "It's okay, buddy. I'll take you outside—"

"You can't," David interrupted. "If the power goes off, the doors automatically lock."

"You mean we're trapped in here?" Sam asked.

Everyone began to murmur. "I'll bet it's the vandal," David said. "He's trapped us down here for some reason. . . ."

Other books in the
wishbone™ Mysteries series:

WISHBONE Mysteries

THE DISAPPEARING DINOSAURS

by Brad Strickland and Thomas E. Fuller

WISHBONE™ created by Rick Duffield

Big Red Chair Books™, *A Division of **Lyrick Publishing**™*

This book is a work of fiction. The characters, incidents, and dialogues are products of the authors' imagination and are not to be construed as real. Any resemblance to actual events or persons, living or dead, is entirely coincidental.

 Big Red Chair Books™, *A Division of **Lyrick Publishing***™
300 E. Bethany Drive, Allen, Texas 75002

©1998 Big Feats! Entertainment

Edited by Kevin Ryan

Copy edited by Jonathon Brodman

Cover concept and design by Lyle Miller

Interior illustrations by Kathryn Yingling

Wishbone photograph by Carol Kaelson

Library of Congress Catalog Card Number: 98-85045

ISBN: 1-57064-337-7

First printing: July 1998

10 9 8 7 6 5 4 3 2 1

To my nephews,
Andrew and Scott

To my nieces, Jennifer and Jessica Fuller—
you're never too old for Wishbone.

FROM THE BIG RED CHAIR . . .

Oh . . . hi! Wishbone here. You caught me right in the middle of some of my favorite things—books. Let me welcome you to the WISHBONE MYSTERIES. In each story, I help my human friends solve a puzzling mystery. In *THE DISAPPEARING DINOSAURS*, I work with my pals David, Sam, and Joe to discover who is trying to destroy the Oakdale College museum's newest prehistoric discovery—the Mundioraptor.

The story takes place early in the fall, just before the events that you'll see in the second season of my WISHBONE television show. In this story, Joe is fourteen, and he and his friends are just starting the eighth grade. Like me, they are always ready for adventure . . . and a good mystery.

You're in for a real treat, so pull up a chair and a snack and sink your teeth into *THE DISAPPEARING DINOSAURS!*

Chapter One

*D*ig, dig, dig, dig, dig!
　　　Wishbone felt the dirt flying out behind him as his front paws churned into the carefully prepared soil of his neighbor Wanda Gilmore's prized rose garden. His paws were a blur, moving so fast even the little brown-and-white-and-black-spotted Jack Russell terrier couldn't see them. It was a warm Friday afternoon in autumn—the perfect weather for one of Wishbone's favorite hobbies.

Dig, dig, dig, dig, dig!

His head was already several inches beneath ground under a rosebush. Occasionally, a small shower of leaves drifted down into the rapidly growing hole, only to erupt again and be scattered behind Wishbone, along with more loose dirt.

Dig, dig, dig, dig . . . Whoa!

Wishbone's head popped out of his excavation site and he looked around. *All right, I know I left it right around here. It was beside the petunias just a minute ago—you just can't trust anyone these days. . . . Aha!* There was his prize, right where he'd left it, lightly spotted with rose petals and bits of bark. He sighed and grinned a big grin.

He pranced over to his bone. *What a bone!* he thought proudly. It wasn't one of those flat, sharp things he got after all the pork chops were eaten; or the round, stubby ones from leftover ham. It was better than either—more mouth-watering than even the almost famous T-bone steak bone; or the equally rare rib bones, with their tangy hint of barbecue sauce!

"Soup bone!" he sang to himself as he nuzzled his new treasure. "Soupy, soupy, soup bone! For Wishbone! A bone to keep and bury deep, oh, life can be so-o-o sweet!" He stared critically down into his new hole. *Not deep enough,* he thought. *Not nearly deep enough for a treasure like this!* The soup bone was almost as tall as he was. He didn't plan to leave it where just any passing mutt might smell it and dig it up. *A dog's gotta defend his bone! It has to be buried very deep! Dig, dig, dig, dig . . .*

A very angry voice yelled at him: "Wishbone! Oh, Wishbone! No!"

Dig, dig, dig, dig, dig!

"Wishbone! Stop that!"

Dig, dig, dig, dig, dig!

"Oh, no! Not the roses! Anything but the roses . . . Wishbone!"

Dig, dig, dig, dig . . . Whoops!

Suddenly, Wishbone felt himself being popped out of his hole as if he were a cork being pulled out of a bottle. Only in his case, it was more like a dog by his collar, he thought. *Okay, so it was exactly like a dog by his collar,* he added silently. He looked up into the frustrated face of Ellen Talbot, his best friend Joe's pretty, brown-haired mother.

"Oh, hi, Ellen." Wishbone grinned hopefully. "You came to help? Great! Better get a shovel, though—you folks aren't built for really serious digging!"

Ellen looked down, shaking her head. "I can't believe you're digging up Wanda's garden again!"

"Actually, it's not so much *again* as *still* . . ."

"And her new rosebushes! She just put them in last week! Oh, she is going to explode when she sees this big gaping hole. Just where did you get that bone?"

Wishbone raced around, did a back flip, and then stood proudly by the gleaming white soup bone. "It's a real beauty, isn't it? This year's model! Note the sleek lines, the bold color. Do I know bones—or do I know bones?"

Ellen stared at the bone and shook her head. "I know exactly where you got it. . . . Joe! . . . Don't you move, Wishbone—you stay right there! . . . *Joe!*"

Wishbone panted happily. "Bones are my life! I even have one in my name."

Ellen called even louder: "Joseph Steven Talbot, I need you out here right now!"

Wishbone looked up in surprise. "Whoa! The *whole* name! Joe must be in some kind of trouble, huh, Ellen?"

The sounds of a screen door slamming and sneakered feet racing across the driveway interrupted Wishbone. He heard Joe call, "I'm coming, Mom! What's all the fuss—" Fourteen-year-old Joe Talbot skidded to a stop, blinking down at Wishbone's wonderful hole. "Oh, no," he finished lamely.

Ellen put her hands on her hips. "Oh, yes! Joe, why did you give Wishbone that bone?"

"I thought you bought it for him," Joe said.

Ellen pushed a strand of hair out of her eye. "I wouldn't mind if he'd chew it inside, but if you give him a bone and let him go outdoors . . . Well, you know he always heads right here with it."

"I know," Joe said. "I think Wishbone believes this is his own private bone bank. Look, you can see more of them down in the hole."

Ellen ran her fingers through her hair and shook her head. "Wanda is going to be furious. She worked so hard on these roses."

Joe looked down at the mound of piled-up dirt, the scattered leaves, the hole, and the tilting rosebush. "Uh . . . maybe we could put everything back the way it was before? The dirt and the bark bits and the roses? That way she wouldn't be upset."

"And she wouldn't chase Wishbone all over the neighborhood the way she did after the gladiolus incident," Ellen said, glancing down at Wishbone, who concentrated on looking innocent.

"I'll do it, Mom," Joe said. He knelt by the hole and

began to shove dirt back around the roots of the rosebush with his bare hands.

"Here," Ellen said, kneeling beside Joe and reaching for the bush. "I'll hold it up straight."

Both of them jumped when they heard Wanda's cheery "Yoo-hoo!"

Wishbone, who had been wisely keeping out of this discussion, cocked his head to one side. He perked up his ears as Wanda Gilmore's classic white 1957 Thunderbird rolled into the driveway of her house. The door swung open and Wanda jumped out. She was clutching three large ring binders to her chest. She smiled and waved broadly at the Talbots, nearly losing one of the binders.

She called again, "Yoo-hoo! Joe and Ellen! You're the very people I wanted to see!"

"Hello, Wanda," Ellen called back brightly. "You're home early."

Wanda charged across the lawn to the garden. She clutched her binders tightly with one hand and pushed her sunglasses into place with the other. "I have the most amazing, the most interesting, news— What are you doing in my garden?"

Wishbone skillfully moved into a spot behind Joe. He nudged Joe's leg. "Okay, here's the plan—you distract Wanda, and I'll grab my bone and run! Okay, Joe?"

"It looks as if Wishbone . . . uh . . . loosened one of your rosebushes," Ellen said apologetically. "We were just steadying it again."

Wanda stared hard at the turned earth, the leaves, the evidence of digging. "He *loosened* my roses?" She shook her head and gave Wishbone a stern look—but a smile kept tugging at the corners of her lips. "Really, Wishbone!"

11

All in all, Wishbone thought as he stared at Wanda, *she's not taking this very well.*

All in all, Joe thought, *she's taking this pretty well.* After her initial shock, Wanda shrugged her shoulders and helped replant the rosebush, much to Joe's relief.

They were sprinkling on the final layer of bark chips when Joe decided it would be a good time to apologize again. "I'm really sorry about all this, Miss Gilmore. Wishbone doesn't dig up your garden on purpose. . . . Well, I guess that he does do it on purpose—but it's nothing personal."

"Don't worry about it, Joe," Wanda said with a laugh, dusting off her hands. "I guess he's just getting into the spirit."

"That's nice of you to say so, Wanda," Ellen said, wiping a speck of black mulch from the tip of her nose. "Getting into *what* spirit?"

Wanda settled back, looked at the bush, and nodded. Then she glanced at Ellen. "Oh, that's right—you don't know the good news yet! It's the most wonderful thing, quite an accomplishment for Oakdale!"

"But you haven't told us, Miss Gilmore," Joe said.

"No, I haven't told you, have I? It's just that I'm so excited! The fossils are going to put the Oakdale College Natural History Museum on the map! The museum will be famous."

Joe frowned. As far as he was concerned, the Natural History Museum was already on the map, as an important part of Oakdale College. It was a popular field-trip location for every school in the area, and it had been for years. "But what do fossils have to do with you not being angry at Wishbone for digging up your garden?" Joe asked.

Wanda blinked at him. "But it's obvious, Joe! Or maybe it isn't, because I still haven't told you. It's like this: Wishbone likes bones. And very old bones turn into fossils. The museum is full of fossils. So Wishbone is getting into the spirit of things by digging up bones, just like Dr. Breckenridge."

"Wanda?" Ellen said. "What bones? What fossils? What Dr. Breckenridge?"

"Dr. *Jonathan* Breckenridge?" Joe asked, feeling excited. "The scientist who writes all those dinosaur books and is an expert on the prehistoric period?"

Wanda laughed. "Yes, Joe, *that* Dr. Breckenridge! The famous paleontologist! He's been on a dig for five years. Thanks to the money given by the Windom Foundation, the museum is getting the results of his work—a brand-new exhibition!" Wanda reached down, scooped up Wishbone's soup bone, and held it over her head as if it were a banner. "Bones! Dinosaur bones! The find of the century!"

"Wow!" Joe said, his head suddenly filled with images of gigantic dinosaur skeletons, frozen in positions of flight and attack. He had really enjoyed reading about dinosaurs and fossil hunters from the time he was about ten years old.

"That's all I can tell you, because I have promised to keep everything else a secret," Wanda said dramatically. "Or at least until tomorrow. Then you can read about it all over the front page of *The Oakdale Chronicle*. The museum said that we could have the story first, before it released the news nationally. Isn't that wonderful?"

"Fantastic!" Ellen said, smiling. "What a great scoop for the paper!"

"But can't you tell us *anything,* Miss Gilmore?" Joe pleaded. "Not even a hint?"

Wanda looked around, as if she suspected spies from other papers might be hiding behind the rosebush. Then she gathered Joe and Ellen around her and lowered her voice to a whisper. "Well, to be perfectly honest, there isn't that much to tell—it seems Dr. Breckenridge is very strict about secrecy. But I can tell you that it involves at least three complete skeletons of what he claims to be a whole new species of dinosaur!"

"Wow! A new kind of dinosaur! . . ." Joe exclaimed, as the roar and thunder of giant lizards filled his head.

Whoa! Wishbone thought, as images of huge dinosaur skeletons as big as houses filled his head. *Serious bones!*

Chapter Two

Wishbone joined in the excitement as the dinosaur skeletons arrived in Oakdale the next Saturday morning. This was a big day for the town. Wanda was president of the Oakdale Historical Society, publisher of *The Oakdale Chronicle,* and a well-known supporter of Oakdale College. She had organized a small ceremony to welcome the fossils and escort them from downtown Oakdale to their new home in the Natural History Museum of Oakdale College.

Wishbone looked around at the crowd that nearly blocked Main Street, and he sighed. Everyone should have known that with Wanda in charge, things wouldn't stay small for long. *But did anyone think to ask the noble dog?* he thought sadly. *Did anyone suggest that a Jack Russell terrier might be a perfect grand marshal for the parade? Nope, not a chance.*

Shading her eyes, Ellen asked Joe, "Do you see Sam anywhere?"

Joe, towering over Wishbone, replied, "No, not yet, Mom."

"I know where she is—over in front of the *Chronicle*

office!" Wishbone dodged through a forest of legs to keep up with Joe and Ellen. "Use your nose, Joe!" He took another deep sniff and filled his head with Scent of Sam. *Yeah, right next to that hot-dog stand. Even humans can smell a hot-dog stand. Speaking of which, I could use a snack.*

"Do you see her yet, Joe?" Ellen asked, as they made their way down the crowded sidewalk.

Joe said, "I can't see *anything* in this crowd, Mom. Who'd have thought this many people in Oakdale were interested in dinosaurs?"

"Dinosaur *bones,* Joe!" Wishbone took another delighted sniff. "Bones that someone had to go out and find—just as I'm about to find Sam for you! Follow the cute little dog!" He suddenly jumped straight up into the air and began to bark loudly. Then he sprinted off into the crowd.

Behind him, Joe groaned, "Oh, Wishbone, not now! Come back, boy!"

Wishbone dashed through the crowd, with Joe and Ellen right behind him. He liked open spaces for a really good run, but a game of dodge-the-legs was fun, too. And the smells! Hot dogs so close he could almost taste the mustard! Cotton candy! Peanuts! And . . . whoa! Someone had dropped half of a perfectly good vanilla-ice-cream cone! Wishbone paused, but he controlled himself and limited the licks to three. He had to stay focused. *Nothing must distract the tracker—Sam comes first; then ice cream next. Wait right there, ice cream!* Wishbone ducked through the crowd and caught sight of Sam. He ran toward her.

Samantha Kepler—"Sam" to her friends—a slim blond girl, saw Wishbone coming and got down on one knee, laughing. "Wishbone! How are you doing?" Sam said. She scratched him behind the ears as she hugged him.

Wishbone was one happy dog. "There, there—yes, right there! Oh, that's good! I'm starting to forget about the ice cream."

"Hi, Joe. Hi, Mrs. Talbot," Sam called, as Joe and his mother joined them.

"Hi, Sam," Ellen said with a smile. "Sorry we're late. We should have followed Wishbone to begin with! He knew exactly where he was going."

Wishbone sat on the sidewalk and scratched his ear with a paw. "Well, Ellen, I was telling you—*Yikes!*" Wishbone had noticed a strange shadow and, looking around, became startled by the sight before him.

Standing next to Sam was a dinosaur!

Actually, Wishbone realized at once, it was a boy dressed in a dinosaur costume. The outfit was bright green, with a long, scaly tail and a huge head filled with teeth. The head had two googly eyes that rolled back and forth whenever it moved. The boy's face glared out from the open mouth of the *Tyrannosaurus rex,* making him look as if he had been swallowed feet first. Wishbone recognized the voice at once—the boy in the costume was Jimmy Kidd, the younger cousin of Damont Jones, a classmate of Joe's.

"You bought me only two hot dogs, Sam. I always eat more than two hot dogs," Jimmy complained.

Sam rolled her eyes. "Your mom said that you had a two-hot-dog limit, Jimmy."

The boy in the dinosaur costume stuck out his lower lip. "No fair, no fair. If Damont was my baby-sitter, he'd let me have more than two hot dogs."

"Well, Damont's not here," Sam told him. "And your mom said two hot dogs only."

Jimmy stuck out his lower lip again. "Then how about an ice cream?"

Joe gave Sam a sympathetic look. "You're baby-sitting Jimmy Kidd?"

Sam shrugged. "Yes. His mom and my mom are friends. She trusts me not to let him eat too much. Damont is grounded again, and I can use the money."

Ellen knelt down in front of the nine-year-old Jimmy and smiled. "Why, James Kidd, is that really you in there?"

The lip was hanging clear down to his chin by now. "'Lo, Mrs. Talbot," he mumbled.

"You know," Ellen said, "I almost thought for a minute you were a real dinosaur!"

Wishbone shook his head in surprise. "Costume or no costume, he smells like Jimmy Kidd!"

The lower lip snapped back into place and Jimmy actually smiled. "It's cool, ain't it, Mrs. Talbot! I'm a *T. rex!* You know what? This costume was used in that really big movie about dinosaurs on that creepy island, and it cost about a hundred million bucks and—"

"It's a beautiful costume, Jimmy," Ellen said. Jimmy beamed at her.

Wishbone was looking at Jimmy and Ellen. *Smooth move, Ellen,* he thought. *Music isn't the only thing that soothes the savage beast—patient listening always works really well, too!*

Sam looked at Joe. "Mrs. Kidd made the outfit for him for last Halloween. When he found out about the parade, he had to wear it, so here we are." She looked at the suit as Jimmy chattered on. "Mrs. Kidd is good at making costumes. She helps out a lot with the Oakdale College Players, the drama group."

"Where's David?" Joe asked. He looked around the crowd, as if he were expecting his other best friend to appear magically. "Isn't he coming?"

"I don't know," Sam answered. "I called to tell him where we'd be. All he'd say was that we'd see him here. He's been really secretive lately. He's doing some kind of a special science project for extra credit, and it's taking up all his free time."

Joe nodded. "That must be why nobody's seen him outside of school for the past couple of weeks. Did he tell you what he's working on?"

"No—that's the secret part. He just says we'll find out when everybody else does. Anyway, he's not the only one working on a project for extra credit." Sam dug into her back pocket and pulled out a well-worn paperback. "Mr. Gurney, over at the used-book store, gave me this when I told him I wanted to read a nineteenth-century British work for extra credit in English class."

Joe looked at the creased and folded cover. *"The Adventures of Sherlock Holmes,"* he read out loud. "That's the first book in which Sherlock Holmes appears as the great detective, isn't it?"

"Right," Sam said, holding the book and thumbing through the worn pages. "It was on the assigned-book list. I remembered you said the stories were even better than the movies, so I thought I'd read them. Holmes was a really cool guy!"

Wishbone perked up. "I know all about Sherlock Holmes!"

Joe said, "Well, Sherlock Holmes is one of the most famous detectives in—"

"Yes, he's great," Sam said with a laugh, interrupting Joe. "But so is Dr. Watson! He's patient and reliable. And he's always ready to help—even when Sherlock doesn't fill him in on the facts of the whole story that they're investigating."

Wishbone stretched. "Well, Holmes once compared

Watson to a 'sturdy English bulldog.' That's a great character reference, if you ask me!" His ears perked up. He heard the sounds of the approaching parade. *Whoops! Soon it's gonna be too late to think about food! I wonder if I could nudge Joe into buying a hot dog for his best friend!*

Boy, what a crowd! Joe thought, as a roar went up from the people lining Main Street. They stood in front of the *Chronicle* building watching the parade. *I'll bet just about everyone in Oakdale is out here.* The *Chronicle* had been full of stories about the Breckenridge expedition for a week. The entire town had been tempted with articles on dinosaur digs, the science of paleontology, and the past work of Dr. Jonathan Breckenridge. The door to the newspaper office opened, and Wanda Gilmore walked out and joined Joe and his group.

"Isn't it thrilling?" Wanda cried over the noise of the assembled crowd.

"Well, it certainly is exciting," Ellen replied.

"I mean from a scientific point of view," Wanda added. "Anyway, I know that this is the biggest parade Oakdale's ever had. I looked it up. The closest we've come to this was when Oakdale High won the state football championship. That was back in 1952, so almost no one remembers it."

"Look at that balloon!" Sam shouted, pointing. "It's huge!" Joe looked up as a gigantic helium balloon came bobbing down Main Street. It was an Apatosaurus—the kind of dinosaur that was once called a Brontosaurus. Its long neck and tail bobbed up and down. It seemed to be nodding in a royal manner at everyone as it soared thirty feet overhead. Students from Oakdale College held ropes that were attached to the balloon and kept it from flying away. The kids were laughing and shouting and trying to stay out of one another's way. The crowd cheered as the balloon floated past. A vendor on one side of the street selling balloons with dinosaurs on them was suddenly doing a lot of business.

"It took me most of the week to arrange for it to be borrowed from that big department store in New York City," Wanda said triumphantly. "I finally asked the Windom Foundation to give the store a call. The next thing I knew, it was on its way."

There was a blast of loud brass music as the Oakdale High School marching band marched into view behind the floating dinosaur. The drill team twirled new white-silk banners with green dinosaurs on them. The band blared out more music as the members marched, and Joe had to smile. The marching band regularly placed in state competitions. Loyal as the citizens in Oakdale were, people went to the high-school football games to see the band's half-time shows—the football team hadn't been to state in a while.

Wishbone started to bark when he saw that the band was followed by a crowd of kids in all kinds of dinosaur costumes—duck-billed Hadrosaurs, spiky-spined Stego-sauruses, even an ostrich-like Struthiomimus. Joe whistled. "Those costumes aren't bad. Someone did a lot of research!"

"I should be out there," grumbled Jimmy Kidd. "My costume's better than any of those."

Joe ignored Jimmy. The costumed marchers ran in and out of the crowd, having a great time. Wishbone barked at them as they ran by. One of them made the dog's day by cringing back, as if he were afraid.

"Hey, Joe, it's Sequoyah!" Sam yelled, grabbing his arm. "It's Sequoyah! Yay, Sequoyah! Go, Bulldogs, go!"

The Sequoyah Middle School marching band made its way up the street behind the dinosaurs. They sounded really great. Their blue-and-gold uniforms sparkled in the sunlight. Joe had to admit they looked good. Then a bulky brown figure burst out of the formation of marchers and the crowd started to cheer.

"Go, Bulldog! Go, Bulldog! Go, Bulldog!" Joe and Sam chanted along with everyone else. The Bulldog mascot of Sequoyah Middle School came bounding down the street. It pranced back and forth across the street in front of the band, punching the air with its forepaws, leading the chants.

"You know, I think that Amanda is the best mascot we've ever had," Sam said.

Joe grinned and nodded. He knew that under the costume was their friend Amanda Hollings. She was a very confident girl with long, black hair. Sam had been the one who'd talked Amanda into trying out for mascot.

"She sure is talented," Joe agreed. He remembered the former Bulldog mascot and added, "Toby is a lot happier working on his science projects. He never really liked being the Bulldog, anyway."

Then Wanda was jumping up and down next to them. "Oh, look, here they come!"

A sleek antique Packard convertible inched along behind the Sequoyah marching band. On the sides of the car were banners with the words "Classic Car Club." Horace Zimmerman, president of the club and a very good friend of Wanda's, steered the motorcar with great care and waved without taking his eyes off the road. A stern-looking middle-aged woman who had white hair and amazingly straight posture sat in the front seat next to him, staring ahead.

"That's Margaret Bradbury," Wanda said with a

knowing nod. "She's the chief executive officer of the Windom Foundation. She's the one responsible for finally getting the dinosaur balloon for the parade."

Neither Joe nor Sam was listening to Wanda. They were both staring at the man in the backseat. He was tall and muscular and dressed all in clean, pressed khaki. His thick blond hair was pulled back into a ponytail, and he wore round, dark glasses. He didn't wave to the crowd, but just nodded as he accepted the cheers.

"That's Dr. Jonathan Breckenridge," Sam whispered to Joe as the Packard passed. "I recognize him from his photos in the newspaper. He's the scientist who led the expedition that discovered the new species."

"And here it comes now!" Joe said, pointing.

An eighteen-wheel tractor-trailer truck rumbled up next. It was flanked on either side by grim-faced security guards on motorcycles. The words "Windom Expeditions" were in large letters across the upper sides of the trailer. The kids lining the sidewalks were most fascinated by the pictures that covered the rest of the truck. The sides of the trailer had been painted so that they looked like slabs of stone. In the "stone" were images of hundreds of dinosaur bones, dominated by two huge skulls with long, sharp teeth.

"Wow!" Sam and Joe said at the same time.

"They're in there!" Joe said, feeling excited. "I'll bet the skeletons are all in there, just waiting to be moved into the museum."

"Is that all?" grumbled a little voice next to them. "That's no big deal—that's just a bunch of dirty old bones. I wanted to see dinosaurs—like in the movies. Who cares about old, dried-up bones? I've found bones like that lots of times in Jackson Park."

"Oh, really?" Sam asked, sounding amused.

"I can find my own old bones. I've done it lots of times," Jimmy Kidd muttered, completely ignored by kids and adults alike. Even Wishbone lay down and put his paws over his ears.

"I wonder why they have all those guards around the truck," Sam said.

Wanda leaned in close. In a loud whisper, she confided, "There's been some trouble. I heard that someone tried to destroy part of the exhibit when it was on the way to Oakdale."

Joe looked at her. "What? Why?"

Wanda shook her head. "I don't have any details, but I did hear that part of one dinosaur was destroyed somehow. The Windom Foundation has hired security guards to make sure it doesn't happen again."

"Hey, look at that!" Sam yelled. "Joe, look at that!"

Joe looked and his mouth fell open. There in the backseat of a car, seated next to a small woman with black hair, David Barnes was waving wildly and wearing a wide grin.

Chapter Three

"Come on!" Sam yelled. She was running up a grassy hill, leading a slow-moving Jimmy Kidd by the hand. "This is a good spot!"

Joe and Wishbone hurried over to her. Joe was looking around at the huge crowd that had gathered in front of the Oakdale College Museum of Natural History. After the parade had passed down Main Street, Ellen had gone back to the library. Wanda said she was going to be part of the group of reporters covering the delivery of the dinosaurs to the museum. Joe and Sam knew they had to find out why David had been in the parade, so they ran to the college campus.

Joe recognized dozens of people from town. They had been joined by hundreds of college students, many of them wearing green-foam-rubber dinosaur hats shaped like the heads of *T. rexes*. Lots of smaller kids gripped the strings of red, yellow, blue, and green balloons that had pictures of Apatosaurs, Stegosaurs, Triceratops, and other dinosaurs on them.

"I'm hot," Jimmy complained.

"You could take off your costume," suggested Sam.

He looked at her, shocked. "No way! This is the best costume here!"

Joe had to agree with that statement as he joined Sam and Jimmy under the shade of a gnarled old oak tree. Jimmy's was the *only* dinosaur costume there. The three of them and Wishbone stood under the oak, on a little rise. The oak provided a good amount of shade. From there they had a good view over the heads of the crowd and the bobbing balloons. The marching bands and costumed mascots had departed.

Joe could see that, in front of the museum, a raised wooden platform about a foot high had been set up. The museum itself was a long, low building of tan brick, with a dramatic glass front. On the platform was a long table covered in a maroon cloth. In the center of the table was a reading stand. It had the Oakdale College seal on it, and it had a silver microphone attached to it. Behind the table sat the people Joe and Sam had seen in the parade down Main Street. These folks were now laughing and talking to one another. Across the front of the table was draped a white-and-blue banner, reading: OAKDALE WELCOMES THE WINDOM EXPEDITION.

The white-haired woman whom Wanda had identified as Margaret Bradbury got up and stood in front of the reading stand. She thumped the microphone to make sure it was on. Joe saw Wishbone flinch a little at the loud *pop!* the thump produced. "Now we know it's on!" said Ms. Bradbury, her voice booming from the speakers. "Can everyone hear me?"

Jimmy yelled, "I can't!"

Someone behind Jimmy and the older kids yelled even louder, "We can hear you fine!"

With a wave, Ms. Bradbury said, "Good! Welcome, everyone, to the Oakdale College campus. This will be the new home of the fabulous creatures discovered by Dr. Jonathan Breckenridge on the Windom Expedition."

Everyone applauded.

The woman waved again and said, "As many of you know, I'm Margaret Bradbury, and I'm here to represent the Windom Foundation. I didn't come here to make a speech, and you didn't come here to listen to me. Let me simply introduce to you the man of the hour. Dr. Jonathan Breckenridge was born in Wyoming. He grew up fascinated by fossils and dinosaurs. He attended Oakdale College. Then he went on to graduate school at both Yale and Harvard. Dr. Breckenridge has been on seven different dinosaur digs in Wyoming, Montana, Canada, and even Africa. Fossils he unearthed can now be seen in New York City's Museum of Natural History; the Smithsonian Institution in Washington, D.C.; and dozens of other museums around the country. We're glad to welcome him back today. Please help me give Dr. Breckenridge a big hand!"

Joe clapped enthusiastically, joining in with the rest of the crowd. He was excited to see Dr. Breckenridge. Joe had just reread *Dinosaur Hunter,* one of the scientist's dinosaur books. It contained lots of photos of the author while on location at different dinosaur digs. Joe guessed that Dr. Breckenridge was about forty-five years old. He was tall, deeply tanned, and he wore his blond hair pulled back in a ponytail. He waved at the crowd, a shy smile appearing on his face.

Jimmy started to say, "*I've* found lots of dinosaurs in Jackson Park—"

Sam whispered, "You need to keep quiet."

On the platform, the scientist slowly stepped up to the microphone and then cleared his throat. After all the applause stopped, he said in a soft voice, "My, I do love dinosaurs. I think everyone does."

The crowd roared in agreement.

Dr. Breckenridge put on a pair of round glasses. Glancing at some notes, he said, "I can't tell you how happy I am to return to Oakdale—and to bring with me some fantastic animals. Thanks to the support of the college and the Windom Foundation, I am able to bring back today fossils from five years full of work in the field. It's by far the longest and the most rewarding expedition I have ever had the good fortune to lead. I want to thank everyone in Oakdale for your wonderful support." His eyes twinkled, and he added, "I think that when the display opens in a few days, you're going to be very pleased. You will be the first members of the public to view a creature that is going to revolutionize the field of paleontology!"

Joe wondered what that remark meant. "Do you suppose that he's *really* found some very strange, unknown species?" he asked Sam.

"I found lots of new species," Jimmy Kidd said. "What are species?"

Sam explained, "It means a new kind of animal or plant." She said to Joe, "Who knows? Maybe he'll tell us. I think the audience is going to ask him some questions."

Sure enough, a small group of reporters were already raising their hands. Dr. Breckenridge called on a young man from WOAK, the Oakdale radio station.

The man said, "Sir, I understand that in addition to your work with actual dinosaurs, you also contributed to a famous computer game about dinosaurs. Could you comment?"

Dr. Breckenridge laughed. "Oh, yes, certainly. Some years back, a computer software company asked me to be the consultant on Bonedig, which is a very popular game among young people."

"Bonedig!" Jimmy said excitedly. "Cool! Damont's got Bonedig Two. Sometimes he lets me play—"

Sam smiled at Jimmy.

Dr. Breckenridge was describing the game. "In the game, the player goes on a dinosaur-hunting expedition and unearths living specimens of dinosaurs. They are fully animated, and a few are pretty dangerous. Some of the game species are real. Others are ones I made up. I will point out that my imaginary dinosaurs' body structures are based on real physical evidence, and on what we know or can guess about what actual dinosaur life was like."

"Do you get any fan letters from kids who play the game?" the reporter asked.

"Sometimes. However, what is more important to me is that the money we make from the game helps us buy much-needed equipment for our digs. And in turn, that equipment has helped us locate more than a dozen rare, well-preserved dinosaur skeletons."

"I bet you that I could win that game in about an hour," Jimmy said. "If Damont ever let me play that long, I sure could."

Joe looked at Sam, who just shrugged.

In a playful tone, the reporter asked, "The game hasn't come true, though, has it? I mean, you've never found an actual living dinosaur, have you?"

Dr. Breckenridge chuckled again. "I promise you, the instant I do, you will be the first to know! No, although I do love to hunt and piece together dinosaur fossils, I have to face the facts. The dinosaurs became extinct sixty-five million years ago, and that's that."

Jimmy tugged at Joe's sleeve.

"What?" Joe asked, looking down at the little boy.

"I bet I could find some dinosaurs that are still

31

alive," Jimmy said. "I'll bet they live down in the bottom of volcanoes."

"Maybe," Joe told him with a grin. "But Dr. Breckenridge doesn't seem to think so."

Joe glanced back up just as the scientist pointed into the crowd and said, "You, young lady—do you have a question?"

The woman at whom Dr. Breckenridge had pointed was quite young, probably in her mid-twenties. She had short dark hair and a trim figure, and she was waving a yellow legal pad.

"Dr. Breckenridge," she said, "my name is Alice Zane, and I'm a newspaper reporter for the Zenith *Times*. I've heard two rumors. One is that you have discovered a whole new species of carnosaur, a meat-eating dinosaur. The second one is that you have some evidence that dinosaurs were a lot more intelligent than most people believe. Would you comment on these items?"

For a moment, Dr. Breckenridge just stared at her. He adjusted his glasses and coughed. Joe saw that the scientist's face was beginning to turn red. "Young lady," he said at last, his voice angry and tight, "I don't choose to comment on either of those two . . . rumors . . . at this time. If you're really interested in my discoveries, I suggest that you come back in a week, when we open the display. I promise you that the announcement I will make then will be newsworthy!"

Joe noticed Wanda Gilmore in the crowd. She was staring at the out-of-town reporter. "I don't think that Miss Gilmore's very happy about that last question," he told Sam.

"It's probably a newspaper thing," Sam replied. "*The Oakdale Chronicle* should be the paper that gets the first opportunity to announce and describe Dr. Breckenridge's discoveries—or that's the way that Miss Gilmore would see it. The *Times* is a much bigger newspaper."

They listened as Dr. Breckenridge told a few stories of the expedition he had led, of the excitement of discovering dinosaur skeletons, and of the extreme care his crew had to use to take the fossilized bones from the rock that contained them.

Jimmy kept interrupting, but Joe still managed to hear Dr. Breckenridge.

At last Dr. Breckenridge concluded, "I think the public has the wrong idea about dinosaur hunting. Most people I talk to seem to think that we paleontologists dig up dinosaurs with spades and pickaxes. That would never do, because the bones are actually very fragile. Usually, we're far more likely to use garden tools and small brooms—sometimes even toothbrushes, so we don't damage even the smallest specimen. So, as you can imagine, digging up a giant animal can take many months—even years—of very hard work!"

Because the people in front of Wishbone were so tall, he couldn't see Dr. Breckenridge. His ears were excellent, though, and he heard every word the scientist said. He sat down and said, "Hey, I know the feeling, Doc! Sometimes it takes me *days* just to locate and dig up a bone I've buried in Wanda's yard. Lots of times I've got to dig all the way through her petunias—her daisies—even her rosebushes! A lot of times, locating the very best bone takes a whole week of serious digging! But when I succeed, it's worth all the time and trouble!"

Dr. Breckenridge's words almost echoed Wishbone's. "In the field, we dinosaur hunters live without television, electricity, and hot water. We're often fifty miles or more from the closest soft bed and hot shower. Most of the time we camp out in tents, eat canned food only, and are subjected to all kinds of foul weather conditions. It's a very rough life in some ways, but when we find a first-class fossil, it's all worthwhile."

Wishbone let his tongue hang out and grinned. "I know what the man means! Dinosaurs! Dinosaur skeletons! Really big bones! Really, really big bones! Gotta find 'em, gotta dig 'em up, gotta bury 'em! Bones are a dog's favorite find!" Wishbone glanced up at Joe, whose eyes were still on Dr. Breckenridge. "Hey, Joe! Are we gonna get to see some really big bones today? Huh? Are we?"

Joe looked down and asked, "What's got you all excited, Wishbone?"

"Bone-talk, Joe! Bones—every dog loves 'em!"

Jimmy looked over at Joe. "How come your dog is whining?" he asked Joe.

Joe shrugged. "Just all the people and the excitement, I guess. Hey, Sam, let's go see if we can find David. I think the speeches are just about over."

"I wanna go see the reporters," Jimmy said. "I'll bet they'll take pictures of me in my costume for the papers. Are there TV cameras down there? It would be so cool to be on TV!"

"If they ask, you can let them take your picture," Sam said.

The crowd began to break up as Joe, Sam, Jimmy, and Wishbone made their way down the hill and across the lawn in front of the museum. Up at the top of the steps, reporters clustered around Dr. Breckenridge and the others at the table, asking questions. Joe saw that Wanda was right there in the thick of things. He smiled, thinking that tomorrow *The Oakdale Chronicle* was bound to have a front-page story on the unveiling of the dinosaurs. Then Joe spotted David. He waved and yelled, and David turned around with an enormous smile on his face.

"Hi!" he said, coming over. "Hey, Jimmy, that's a cool costume."

"It was in the movies," Jimmy said.

Joe grinned at David. "What's going on?" he asked. "How did you get to ride in the parade?"

"You didn't tell us you were going to do that!" Sam added.

David grinned. "It was a surprise. Remember how I won the regional competition in CAD?"

"What's that?" Jimmy asked.

"Computer-assisted design," David explained. "It's when you use a computer to draw blueprints, plans, or sketches. You can even animate them. Well—"

"I do that all the time," Jimmy said. "I helped draw the dinosaurs for Bonedig."

David shook his head. "Well, I'm getting to do something like that. I get to be an intern at the museum for the next month. Dr. Maddy Kingston is in charge of the museum's computers, and I'm on the team designing an interactive dinosaur exhibit."

"No way!" Sam said. "What will it be like?"

"Well," David said, "some parts will be animations of the way the dinosaurs looked in real life. Sometimes you can use the computer to learn about the dinosaurs—like what food they would eat, what kind of nest they would make, what their eggs would look like. Stuff like that. Every-thing will be in full color, with super-stereo sound. And the neatest thing is this." David took a little leather case from his pocket and opened it. Inside was a gleaming silver badge inscribed with the words OAKDALE COLLEGE MUSEUM OF NATURAL HISTORY STAFF. "I can go everywhere inside the museum," David said. "Even places most people can't—the storage rooms, the preparation rooms, and, of course, the computer lab. Want to see where I'll be working?"

"Sure," Joe said enthusiastically. "Can Wishbone come with us?"

"Hey," David said, "I've got the badge. Sure he can!"

Wishbone wagged his tail gleefully. "Bones! We're gonna see bones! Let's go, gang!" He trotted along as David led Joe, Sam, and Jimmy into the museum. David opened a door marked "Staff Only," and they walked down a long corridor.

Wishbone's nose twitched at all the new aromas—chemicals, packing materials, plastics, a security guard . . . Whoa!

A tall, muscular man wearing the uniform of a museum guard stepped out of a doorway and said, "Excuse me, but you shouldn't be here."

David stopped and said, "It's okay, Mr. McIntyre. These are my good friends. Guys, this is Mr. Benjamin McIntyre. He's head of security here."

Wishbone sat up straight. "Nice to meet you, sir!"

The guard shook his head. "David, I know *you* have clearance, but your friends don't—and I *know* the dog doesn't have a badge."

Wishbone blinked. "My license! I have my license! Right here on my collar. See?"

"But I just want to show them where I work," David explained to the guard.

Mr. McIntyre shook his head. "Someone phoned in a threat about destroying the dinosaur exhibit. Security is really tight right now," he said.

Wishbone thought Joe sounded startled when he asked, "*Destroy* the exhibit? Who would do something like that?"

"We don't know," replied Mr. McIntyre, "but we're not taking any chances. David, if you want to take your friends through, you'll have to get permission from Dr. Kingston. Okay?"

David sighed. "Okay. Come on, guys. Sorry. Maybe another time."

Jimmy said, "My cousin Damont wouldn't let anybody push him around. He'd get us in."

Wishbone glanced back at Jimmy, waddling down the corridor in his dinosaur suit. The Jack Russell terrier gave his head a good shake. "David will get us in next time. He's pretty smart for a human. And let's face it—I hear destiny calling me! This dog has a date with some serious bones!"

Chapter Four

Later that afternoon, Joe was at home reading one of his dinosaur books when the phone began to ring. "I'll get it!" he called to his mom. He hurried to pick up the phone, with Wishbone right at his heels.

"Hi, Joe," said David, as soon as Joe had lifted the receiver. "You busy?"

"No. Why?"

"If you want to come and tour the museum, I've got your badge," David replied. "I've got one for Sam, too."

Wishbone pawed at Joe's leg. He looked down and grinned. "Can Wishbone come, too?" Joe asked. "I'll watch after him and keep him out of trouble."

"Let me ask Dr. Kingston. Just a minute."

Joe heard David talk to someone.

Then David was back on the phone. "She says it's fine, but she'd like him to be on a leash. Okay?"

"Great," Joe said. "When should we be there?"

"Right now," David said. "I'll call Sam."

Joe hurried to find his mom. He explained about David and the badges and asked if he could go to the museum.

"Of course," Ellen said. "I think you'll really enjoy yourself."

"Thanks, Mom," Joe said. He went and got Wishbone's leash. "David says Wishbone can come, too, if I put his leash on him."

"Keep him away from the fossils," Ellen said with a smile. "I don't think Wanda would like it if he dug a hole big enough to bury a Triceratops!"

Joe rode his bike downtown, with Wishbone running alongside. Joe was always amazed at Wishbone's energy. The Jack Russell terrier loved to rush along at top speed. His tongue hung out and his ears flapped in the wind.

Before long, Joe turned onto the Oakdale College campus. He parked his bike at the rack beside the front steps of the Natural History Museum. He snapped the leash onto the collar of a grinning, panting Wishbone just as Sam rode up on her own bike.

"Hi!" she said, climbing off and then bending over to ruffle Wishbone's ears.

"I guess we just go in the front entrance," Joe said.

A security guard sat at a desk just inside the front door. He used a walkie-talkie to speak to someone. After a few seconds, the "Staff Only" door opened, and David came out to meet them, smiling.

"Hi, guys," he said, holding out a couple of shiny gold-colored plastic name badges. "Here you go."

Joe took one and saw that it had "Joe Talbot" printed on it. Beneath that was the word "Guest." He pinned it to his shirt as Sam attached her own name badge. "This is great," Joe said. "Have there been any more threats?"

David looked concerned. "Actually, I think there have been. I know Mr. McIntyre is taking everything pretty seriously." Then he brightened up. "Do you want to see the main exhibit? The staff is still putting the skeletons together, so we have to be careful."

"Sure!" Sam said. "Let's go."

David led them through a hall with dioramas of prehistoric life built into the walls. Then he opened a big set of double doors. Joe blinked. The hall they walked into had eight sides, with a roof made of glass, so that light flooded everything. A security guard looked at them sharply, spotted their badges, then waved them past. Joe craned his neck to try to see the dinosaurs, but to his disappointment, he could see very little.

In the center of the hall, supported by wires attached to a steel framework that ran beneath the skylights, were parts of dinosaurs. David said there were six. Unfortunately, most of the skeletons were concealed by green-cloth curtains hung on rolling metal frames. Joe could hear people talking behind the screens, and he could glimpse a few bones above the screens. Otherwise, there was little to see. "They're sure keeping everything top secret," he said.

"Dr. Breckenridge's orders," said David. "Until he makes his big announcement, he doesn't want anyone to see the fully assembled skeletons."

"What *is* his big announcement?" Sam asked.

David gave her an apologetic look. "I can't tell anyone," he said. "They trust me here."

"Sure they do," Joe told him. "You always do a great job, David."

"Thanks, guys— Uh-oh! Stay still, everyone. Joe, maybe you'd better pick up Wishbone."

Joe stooped and lifted Wishbone, who squirmed in his grasp. Then he saw why David was concerned. Ben McIntyre had come around from the back of the hall, and he was holding four dogs on a leash. Four *big* dogs, Joe noticed. They were black Dobermans, straining at their leashes. The animals were sleek-coated and muscular, and their expressions were anything but friendly.

"Boy!" Joe muttered. "They look mean!"

"They're security dogs," David explained. In a louder voice, he called, "Hi, Mr. McIntyre! My friends have clearances."

Mr. McIntyre commanded the dogs. "Sit!" he said sharply. The four Dobermans immediately obeyed, in perfect unison. "Hi, kids," Mr. McIntyre said. "Okay, just stand there and let Groucho, Chico, Harpo, and Zeppo sniff you, and you'll be all right. Keep a good hold on the little dog, son."

Joe held Wishbone tight as the four dogs came over and sniffed at him and Sam. "How can you tell them apart?" he asked. "They all look exactly alike to me."

"Look closer," Mr. McIntyre told him. "Groucho has the dark eyebrows. Chico has larger brown spots around his eyes. Harpo has the longest legs. Zeppo's the smallest. They really are brothers, by the way. That's why they're named after the famous old-time comedy team of the Marx brothers."

With a chuckle, David said, "I know what you're thinking—the Marx brothers were comedians, and these dogs don't look like they've even *got* a sense of humor. Still, they're good security. Once they know you, they won't bother you."

Joe said, "Mr. McIntyre, it looks like the museum is taking the threats pretty seriously."

Mr. McIntyre nodded. "We have to, son. Whoever's made the phone threat has been disguising his voice—or maybe even *her* voice. Anyway, from what the person has said, we know that he or she has a good idea of the museum's operation and layout. The last thing we want is for some nut to damage the valuable exhibit. David, I'm going to go on now and let the dogs get used to the place. You can take your friends on your tour."

"Okay, thanks," David said. He smiled with pride at the responsibility he had been given.

Once the Dobermans were safely past, Joe put Wishbone down. Wishbone turned to watch the retreating Dobermans.

Joe tugged at his dog's leash, and Wishbone fell into step beside him. David led them into an open elevator, touched a button, and they went down one floor. As the elevator door opened, David explained, "This is the main basement area. A lot of the prep rooms are here."

"Prep rooms?" Sam asked.

David nodded. "Preparation rooms," he explained. "This is where the exhibits are put together—at least the ones that aren't as big as dinosaurs! There are some storage rooms, too. More of them are one floor below us, in the sub-basement. This part isn't open to the public, so it isn't as nice as the rest of the museum, but it's pretty functional."

David looked around. The walls were built of concrete blocks, painted a light cream color. The lights were fluorescent fixtures that did nothing to make the halls beautiful, but he liked the place. He thought it had a neat, professional look. That thought made David feel more professional himself.

David showed Sam, Joe, and Wishbone a couple of rooms where smaller exhibits were put together or repaired. Then he led them to a glass door reinforced with wire. "I work in there," he told them, pointing inside. "This is the computer center. Let me introduce you to my supervisor first."

They went through the doorway and down a short corridor. Then they went through a second set of doors.

David knocked on a door, and a woman's voice called, "Come in!"

David led the way. He smiled as he saw his boss. She was a thin, short woman, in her early forties, who had an explosion of black hair. She sat at a computer monitor. She stood up and put on a pair of black-rimmed glasses that had been dangling from a cord around her neck. She was wearing jeans and a T-shirt with a cartoon-style drawing of a Triceratops—a tanklike dinosaur with three huge horns on its head and a big bony frill on its neck. But this particular Triceratops was in show business. It reared on its hind legs, tap-dancing. In one front paw it held a cane, and in the other a straw hat. It had a big, goofy smile on its face that made David grin, too.

David introduced the woman as Dr. Maddy Kingston. She shook hands with Joe and Sam. "*Dr. Kingston* makes me feel all stiff and formal," she told them. "Just call me Maddy. Want to see our lab?"

"Sure!" Sam said.

"Come on, then. I'll give you the fifty-cent tour," Maddy said with a laugh. She stooped and ruffled Wishbone's ears. "This must be Wishbone. I've heard a lot about you!"

David laughed. "Watch out for Wishbone," he warned in a teasing voice. "He's nice, but before you know it, you're feeding your lunch to him!"

"I've already eaten my lunch today," Maddy said, winking at everyone.

They went into another room. This one was the size of a classroom. A dozen computers hummed and beeped and blipped as young people tapped on their keyboards.

"Here's my station," David said, smiling as he sat down. "Watch this." He began to type commands into the keyboard. "When the exhibit opens," he said, "there'll be computers and monitors out in the main hall. You can stop at them and follow some simple directions to do what I'm doing now. But at this stage here, it isn't so simple, because I'm still designing it. Now, watch."

The blue screen flickered and a picture appeared. David nodded toward the landscape of dry, bare hills.

"This is supposed to be the dig site," he explained. "Now, a visitor will just have to touch the screen to make this happen, but right now I still have to type in a command. Here we go, hunting for dinosaurs."

He typed some more, and the picture changed. Now everyone saw a cutaway version of the hill, as if it had been sliced in two and they could see right inside it.

Far below the surface lay a jumble of bones. "Is that the dinosaur?" Joe asked. "What kind is it?"

"That's the trick," David answered, pleased at Joe's interest. "Once the program's running correctly, you'll be able to 'dig' out the bones, one at a time, by touching them and dragging them to the surface. Then you'll have to put them together. At this point you'll be able to identify the creature. I'll have to cheat a little on this, but here's what it would look like."

David typed in a command. Then, in jerky movements, the bones collected themselves into a pile. Next, they began to assemble themselves—the foot bones became connected to the leg bones, which connected to the hip bones, and so on. After about a minute, a two-legged dinosaur skeleton stood upright on the screen.

"It's a duckbill," Joe said.

Maddy chuckled. "Right, except the scientific name is *Hadrosaur*. This is the kind called a Maiasaurus. Show them the next stage, David."

"Okay," David replied. "This is the last working stage right now, but there'll be more later. Watch." He entered

another command. The dinosaur skeleton began to move,
as if it were walking across a prehistoric landscape.

Joe said, "Neat! What will the next stage be?"

David was happy that Joe and Sam liked his project,
but he knew a lot of work still lay ahead. "Eventually, the
program will end up with the dinosaur being re-created.
You'll see the muscles form, then the skin, and then
you'll have an animation of the way the animal looked in
life. That'll take more programming, though."

"It looks really great already," Joe said. Then he
turned to Dr. Kingston. "Dr.—uh . . . I mean, Maddy,
what about that phone threat Mr. McIntyre mentioned?
Do you think someone actually wants to destroy the
exhibit?"

Maddy crossed her arms and frowned. "I don't know.
Dr. Breckenridge certainly takes the threat very seriously.
He paid out of his own pocket to have some trained guard

dogs brought in. And someone has damaged the fossils from this exhibit already."

"What?" Sam asked. "How? What happened?"

Maddy shrugged. "The tractor-trailer that was transporting the fossils to Oakdale was vandalized. One night the truck driver parked in a motel lot so he could get some sleep. Someone broke the lock on the trailer and smashed important parts of the fossils—the forelimb bones, to be exact. Dr. Breckenridge insisted on actually having someone stationed on night-watch duty in the truck after that. Then yesterday was the phone threat that Mr. McIntyre mentioned. It was a muffled voice that whispered, 'I've destroyed part of the bones already. Before I'm done, I'll smash the rest of them to powder, too.' We have to take that threat seriously."

David nodded. He remembered how upset Dr. Breckenridge had sounded when he was showing the museum staff the wreckage—crumbled, smashed rock that could never be reassembled. Dr. Breckenridge had taken a deep interest in David's work, and David liked him a lot. Just seeing the scientist's disappointment made David all the more determined to do everything he could to help Dr. Breckenridge.

"We all take the threat seriously," David told Joe and Sam. "That's why I'm happy that Groucho, Chico, Harpo, and Zeppo are around. I don't think they'd let anyone that should not be here get past them." He reached down and scratched Wishbone's head. "They're as protective of these bones as Wishbone is of the ones he buries in Miss Gilmore's yard!"

Wishbone stuck out his tongue and gave a wide doggie grin that made David—and everyone else—laugh out loud.

Chapter Five

Joe always had a wonderful time at Pepper Pete's. The food was tasty, of course, but he liked the smell of the restaurant, too. He took a deep sniff as he, Sam, David, and Wishbone came into the pizza parlor and made their way to their special table in the back.

Sam pulled out a chair and said, "Okay, the first thing you need to know is that my dad's been experimenting with the pizzas again."

Joe and David looked at Sam, who shrugged.

"I thought you said the Super-Extra-Large Triple Pepperoni Special was his last experiment," Joe said.

"Well . . ."

"Yeah, Sam, you said he couldn't make them any larger unless he got a bigger oven," David interrupted. "And remember what happened when he tried for the *Quadruple* Pepperoni Special? No matter how much cheese he put on it, pieces of pepperoni fell off every time you tried to lift a slice."

"Actually, that one was kind of neat," Joe said with a laugh, as he remembered the thick, spicy creation. "It was so packed with stuff that you had to cut it up with a knife and fork and hold the pieces together with toothpicks!"

"Actually, the only one who thought it was *really* neat was Wishbone," said a deep male voice from behind them. The kids turned just in time to see Walter Kepler, Sam's father and the owner of Pepper Pete's, come bustling out from behind the counter. He held a steaming pizza in a pan high over his head with one hand, and a stack of plates in the other. "My customers aren't used to eating pizza with a knife and fork. Half the time it all ended up on the floor, and a certain Jack Russell terrier made sure it didn't stay there long."

"Hi, Dad!" Sam said with a smile.

"Hello, Sam. Hi, kids. And hello to you, Wishbone." Mr. Kepler placed the pizza expertly down on the center of the table, then stacked the plates next to it. "How was the field trip to the museum?"

"It was great, Mr. Kepler," Joe said. "We got to see the computer center, where David works."

Mr. Kepler nodded. "Right. Sam told me all about that. Congratulations, David!"

David grinned back at him. "Thanks."

"In order to celebrate, I'd like you to try my new recipe. Here you are, kids—this is the very first Pepper Pete's Perfect Paramount Pizza!"

"Wow!" all three kids exclaimed together. The Perfect Paramount Pizza steamed up at them, all golden bubbling cheese and still-simmering tomato sauce. It smelled magnificent but looked somehow . . . strange.

"Uh . . . Dad," Sam said. "Isn't it a little lumpy?"

Mr. Kepler raised his eyebrows. "They're *good* lumps, Sam. This pizza includes everything that anyone has ever even *thought* should be on top of a pizza! Well, enjoy! I've got other customers to wait on!" Mr. Kepler headed in the direction of the kitchen. Then paused and called over his shoulder, "I'll need a full report from you."

"Sure thing, Dad," Sam called back. Then she turned to her friends. "All right, guys, eat up, but be careful. This looks like another of Dad's knife-and-fork creations."

Joe slid one of the thick, wedge-shaped slices onto his plate. Taste exploded from it as soon as he bit down into it. "Mmm . . . chicken, and . . . meatball! Hey, this is delicious, Sam!"

Sam bit into her own slice and chewed thoughtfully. "Dad tries hard—I think he's really outdone himself with this one."

"Me, too," David chimed in. "I think I just bit into a water chestnut. Weird! But good!"

For a few minutes, Joe and his friends just enjoyed Mr. Kepler's new pizza. Finally, Sam put down her piece and frowned.

"Something wrong, Sam?" David asked.

Sam shook her head slowly. "Just something about this afternoon that's been bothering me."

"I bet I know," David said. "The vandalism and the telephone threat."

"No, not that," Sam replied. "The exhibits. I don't see how fossils could be assembled like that. Wouldn't bones that had turned to rock be too brittle?"

David was just about to answer her, but Joe cut in. "You're right, Sam. Fossils are way too fragile for that. The bones that are being put together in the museum are really what's called *casts*. See, the technicians make molds from the original fossils. Then they pour liquid resin into the molds. Resin is a liquid plastic that dries into a hard solid. When it hardens, the workers take it out of the molds. At that point, they have a perfect, full-sized model of the bones."

David stared at him. "How did you know that?"

Joe took another bite of pizza. *Wow—roast beef!* he thought. When he had finished chewing, he said, "Come on, David. You remember what my room was like when I was Jimmy Kidd's age—you slept over enough."

David laughed and slapped his head. "Of course— How could I have forgotten that?"

"Forgotten *what?*" Sam asked in a puzzled voice.

Joe slipped Wishbone a piece of pizza and said, "When I was a little kid, I had all sorts of dinosaur stuff— pictures, books, posters, models, dioramas. If it had a dinosaur on it, I owned it. I even had dinosaur sheets."

Sam nodded. "Wow! Talk about being a collector!"

Joe ate some more pizza, then said, "Anyway, the skeletons at the museum are lightweight resin casts of the fossils. I read about that in my books."

"Joe's right, Sam," David said. He leaned forward, his eyes bright with excitement. "Dr. Breckenridge came in one afternoon and talked to the staff for about three hours. He explained the whole process. I thought finding the fossils was difficult! But that's only the beginning! Once the fossil hunters find them, they have to start picking the bones out of the rocks—*very* carefully. It can take almost forever. I mean, they have to be *really* careful. He showed us a picture of a chunk of rock with some bones from a small dino all jumbled up in it. Then he showed us another picture of the fossils after they'd been removed. They were tiny, barely a handful."

"The rock that contains all the bones is called the *matrix,*" Joe explained. "And to get the fossils out, the scientists have to use soft brushes, small hammers, picks, and chisels, and even dentist's tools."

"Dr. Breckenridge let us all work on little fossils," David said. "I had a shark's tooth embedded in limestone.

It took me an hour just to get the surface exposed, but Dr. Breckenridge said I was doing a good job."

Joe saw how bright his friend's eyes were. He said, "You really like Dr. Breckenridge, don't you, David?"

"Working with him is almost as cool as working with Maddy," David explained. "I mean, he went out and actually found all this stuff."

Sam said, "All right, I understand about the bones and molds and the casts. After that, what happens to the *real* fossils?"

Joe had a quick answer for that, too. He said, "They're labeled and stored so they can be used as parts of other exhibits. Or sometimes they're used for resource material to reconstruct other dinosaur skeletons."

"*Other* dinosaurs?" Sam asked with a frown. "Why wouldn't museums just use the original skeletons?"

"Because you hardly ever find a complete skeleton," David explained. "You have to piece together the bones you have. After that, you kind of create what's missing. If you have all the bones of the left leg, you can pretty much figure out what the right leg bones were like, and go from there."

"But isn't that cheating?" Sam asked, pushing her plate away.

"Nope," David said grandly, gesturing with a forkful of pizza. "That's science."

Joe glanced over at Sam and noticed that she was only half listening. She seemed to be dividing her attention between the boys' conversation and a well-worn paperback book that she was holding just out of sight under the table.

"Are we boring you?" Joe teased.

Sam shrugged. "No. I'm just trying to keep up with my extra-credit reading."

David asked, "You still reading Sherlock Holmes?"

Sam laughed. "I'm finally starting to understand what Dr. Watson saw that was special in Sherlock Holmes. He's a real genius, and he sees everything. Nothing escapes him at all. So far, the story is really interesting."

"For required reading," Joe replied with a smile.

"Right. It's a pity that Sherlock Holmes wasn't a real person. I'll bet he could figure out who made that threat and vandalized the exhibition."

Joe leaned back in his chair. "Oh, he'd probably just look at you and say something like 'Elementary, my dear Samantha.'"

"E-gad! Holmes, do you really think so?"

The three friends began to laugh. When Walter Kepler looked over at them, he grinned broadly. "I take it the pizza's a huge success!" he called to them.

"It sure is," David called out. Sam and Joe were still too busy laughing to respond.

Wishbone's tail thumped. He was in the Talbots' dining room. "Tell her about the dogs, Joe! Tell her about the dogs!"

Wishbone sat attentively next to the dining room table. His head moved back and forth as he watched Joe and his mother discussing the kids' adventures at the museum.

"It was great, Mom! David took us on a tour of where the computer staff is working on the interactive program. We actually got to see a preview of how it works! Talk about *neat!*"

Wishbone wriggled as he remembered the museum. "Tell her about the dogs, Joe! They've got dogs working there! Right there in the museum! Dobermans! Of course, it would be a lot neater if they were Jack Russells—and I am referring specifically to me!"

Joe said, "Security is really tight, Mom. The museum has these guard dogs—four Dobermans—and they had to smell us so they'd know who we were and everything!"

Wishbone grinned, his tongue hanging out. "Okay, that's the dogs. Now tell her about the bones!"

"Did you get to see the actual exhibit?" his mother asked as she began to set the table for a late dinner. "The actual bones?"

Wishbone blinked. "You read my mind, Ellen!"

"Oh, Mom, they don't display the *real* bones," Joe said, moving to help his mother with the plates. "They had everything hidden behind huge green curtains hung from rolling frames. But you could see shadows of people moving around back there when the light hit them just right. There wasn't enough light there to see the dinosaur skeletons, though."

Ellen patted Joe's arm. "Just be patient. They'll have everything all ready to display soon enough. Then you can see the exhibit just the way it's meant to be."

"I suppose so," Joe said with a sigh. "I just don't like having to wait until it's all finished."

Ellen smiled. "You're not alone. Most of Oakdale is waiting for the exhibition to open. I don't think there is a single book left on dinosaurs in the library. We've begun to request them through inter-library loans now. It's because Wanda's running all those promotional stories in the *Chronicle*. She's certainly helping to heighten the interest in the show."

"Miss Gilmore always knows how to do that kind of publicity," Joe agreed. "What's for dinner, Mom?"

"I got a very nice pot roast from Beck's Grocery. The shop is running a . . . what did Mr. Beck call it? . . .

Oh—a Mastodon Meat Marathon Sale. He's having that in honor of the exhibition."

Joe frowned. "Uh . . . Mom, mastodons are not dinosaurs. They're extinct mammals, related to modern elephants."

Ellen surveyed the table and nodded. "I know that, Joe, and I think Mr. Beck does, too. He just wanted to come up with something that would catch people's interest. He couldn't come up with a dinosaur that started with *m*. Speaking of which, is Wishbone's doggie door locked?"

Joe blinked. "What?"

Wishbone gave Ellen a startled look. "Locked? My doggie door? You mean I'm a prisoner?"

Ellen sighed. "I'll go lock it." She went into the kitchen. Then she came back a few moments later with something hidden behind her back.

Wishbone's mouth was watering. "That's a very familiar smell, Ellen. Come on—what is it?"

Ellen said, "Wishbone, I hope you enjoy this—though you're not going to get a chance to bury it!" Ellen handed Wishbone what she had been hiding.

Wishbone's eyes popped open wide. "It's a bone. And *what* a bone!"

"Wow, Mom!" Joe exclaimed. "That thing's huge!"

"It might be a mastodon bone—at least it was part of the sale at Beck's." She grinned and patted Wishbone on the head. "Enjoy it, Wishbone."

Wishbone grabbed the bone in his mouth and raced to his big red chair. *Okay, I can't bury it in Wanda's garden. Well, then, I'll just go for my second choice—I'll hide it under the cushion. But first . . .* He circled three times and settled down to some serious chewing.

Pretty good, pretty good. Of course, it isn't a dinosaur bone, but it'll do. As Wishbone chewed, he thought about

all the events that had been happening. Ellen's story about the big sale at Beck's proved there was a lot of excitement in the air about Dr. Breckenridge's mysterious exhibition. *I hope it opens soon,* Wishbone thought. *I really want to check out those bones. What kind of troublemaker would smash apart perfectly good bones?*

The image of the four Doberman Marx brothers—Groucho, Harpo, Chico, and Zeppo—floated through his mind. *I've gotta admit—those guys sure look like guard dogs. But it takes more than looks and brawn to get the job done. If someone is really trying to destroy the exhibition, it's gonna take a major amount of brains to stop the culprit.*

There was no doubt in Wishbone's sharp mind about who those brains belonged to. He was the best guard dog in Oakdale. He knew what he had to do.

Defend those bones!

Chapter Six

"I'm off to pick up Sam, Mom," Joe called as he raced out the back door on Monday afternoon.

"Ride carefully," his mother called. "And be back in time for dinner."

Joe called back, "Don't worry, Mom! Come on, Wishbone. We've got things to do!" With that, he was on his bicycle and racing out of the driveway, Wishbone hot on his wheels.

It was a marvelous Indian-summer kind of day. Autumn was coming, but summer was not quite gone. The air was still warm, but Joe thought it had a crisp bite to it, like a tart apple. Joe pedaled out of his neighborhood and rode into downtown Oakdale. Before he knew it, he was flying past the post office, and the wind created by his speed blew his hair out of his face. He passed Sequoyah Middle School, on his left, then headed over to Main Street. It was hard to believe that just two days ago he and his friends had stood in the same place to watch the parade that marked the arrival of Dr. Breckenridge and his wonderful dinosaur exhibition—whatever it was. Now David had invited him, Sam, and Wishbone to see the latest work on the interactive program.

The next thing Joe knew, he and Wishbone were coming up on Pepper Pete's. Sam stood out front next to her bike, waving her baseball cap. As soon as she was sure Joe had seen her, she jumped on her bike and took off up Main Street. Joe and Wishbone didn't even slow down. Sam wanted to race, and when Sam Kepler wanted to race—well, all you could do was race!

The friends sped past Beck's Grocery and the Dart Animal Clinic, pedaling as hard as they could. They took just a second to throw a wave at Rosie's Rendezvous Books & Gifts, just in case Mr. Gurney or Dr. Quarrel were taking a break from their everlasting chess games. Then they whizzed past the offices of *The Oakdale Chronicle* and swung a right around Snook's Furniture. Finally, they headed up the gentle slope to Oakdale College. Traffic was light, and they were careful to stay on the right side of the street. Joe had been staying behind but caught up with Sam as they were passing the Oakdale lake.

Sam leaned even farther over her handlebars, her legs pumping up and down. With a final burst of energy, both riders raced through the gray-granite pillars that marked the entrance to the college. Wishbone bounded along just behind them.

They finally pulled up under the gnarled old oak tree near the museum. Wishbone trotted up and settled down between the two friends, tongue hanging out and sides heaving. His whole body seemed to radiate his excitement.

Suddenly, Joe looked up and grabbed Sam's arm. "Hey, look! Something's going on over at the museum!"

A small red sports car was parked in the street in front of the museum. In front of the gleaming double doors to the building, two familiar figures were shouting at each other.

Startled, Joe exclaimed, "It looks like that reporter from Zenith is having an argument with Ben McIntyre!"

"I wonder what's up," Sam said. They looked at each other. Then, in an instant, they were wheeling their bicycles toward the museum, with Wishbone loping along beside them.

Ben McIntyre stood there, blocking the entrance through the doors. His arms were crossed over his massive chest. The young woman Joe recognized as Alice Zane, the reporter from the Zenith *Times,* was in front of the security guard. Both looked less than happy.

"But you can't *do* this!" Alice was arguing. "You're interfering with the freedom of the press!"

Mr. McIntyre replied, "Miss Zane, freedom of the press does not include the right to make irresponsible, unreliable statements in the media."

"Unreliable!" Alice shouted. "Every word I wrote in my story was based on absolute fact, and you know it!"

Joe and Sam stood a few steps away from the two, listening to the angry words.

Ben McIntyre said, "Both Oakdale College and the Windom Foundation asked you not to mention the telephone threat and vandalism until our investigation is completed." Ben McIntyre held up a copy of the Zenith *Times.*

Joe read the headline:

DINOSAUR EXHIBITION DAMAGED BY MYSTERY VANDAL!
THREAT CONTINUES AGAINST MUSEUM AND STAFF

Alice Zane put her hands on her hips. "My paper had every right to publish that story. The public has the right to know what's been going on here!"

Mr. McIntyre folded the paper. "I am sure it does.

However, because of the bad publicity you've given us, I'm equally sure that Oakdale College has the right to prohibit you from attending today's special preview for members of the press and dignitaries."

"Oakdale College—ha!" snapped Alice, her dark eyes flashing. "Oakdale College had nothing to do with this! This has the Windom Foundation written all over it. Not to mention the great Dr. Jonathan Breckenridge! I'm going to call my editor right away—"

"Your editor, Mr. Conner, has already phoned us," Mr. McIntyre said. "He's promised to see that your future stories won't be as sensational as this one was."

Alice's face burned a bright red. "What!"

Mr. McIntyre held up a hand. "The college doesn't want any more trouble because of you. I can admit you if you'll agree to follow our rules. You'll just need to see Margaret Bradbury, of the Windom Foundation." He shrugged. "After all, the local paper here in Oakdale reported the same things you did, Miss Zane. But it didn't make it seem as if some crazy person is threatening the entire museum and everyone in it. All we ask from you is a little self-control."

"Self-control!" Alice said, glaring at Mr. McIntyre.

"That's right," Ben McIntyre said in a calm voice. "Until you show a little self-control, I guess you just won't be able to write any more stories about this event."

"This isn't fair!" Alice sputtered. "I'm going to talk to that reporter from the *Chronicle*—that Miss Gilmore. When people in this town find out how you're trying to interfere with the freedom of the press—"

"I have a job to do here, Miss Zane," Ben replied quietly. "I'm not paid to take chances with my employers' security. I respect your right to report the news. And I'm sure Miss Gilmore will agree. But you could learn a valuable lesson from her about how to write a story that sticks only to the facts. Good day." Mr. McIntyre turned and marched back into the museum. He locked the double doors behind him with a dull, but very noticeable, click.

Alice turned and saw Joe and Sam. "He's not going to get away with this!" she said angrily. "Something strange is going on in there. I know it! And I'm going to find out what it is!"

Joe, Sam, and Wishbone watched as Alice climbed into her sports car, wheeled away from the museum, and disappeared through the granite pillars.

"Wow!" Sam whispered. "Poor Miss Zane."

"Come on, Sam," Joe said, wheeling his bicycle around the museum toward the security entrance and pinning his Guest badge on his shirt. "Let's see if we can get inside to see David. I'll bet that he knows what's really going on here."

"I'm starting to think nobody does," Sam muttered as she followed him. Wishbone trotted along beside her.

Maddy Kingston was sitting hunched over her computer terminal when Wishbone followed Joe and Sam into the interactive project work room. His nose was busy sniffing. *Whoa, Maddy!* he thought, staring up into her serious face. *You're looking a bit tense.* Wishbone glanced around the large room. Each terminal had a technician or graphic artist glued to it. Every few seconds one of them would groan and slip a disk in or out of a drive. *Correction. Everyone in here* is *tense!* Wishbone thought.

Wishbone could sense how tired everyone was as he trotted from work station to work station. Finally, he went back to where Joe and Sam were standing by

David. *David doesn't look happy, either. Something really bad is happening here.*

David sat slumped in a chair, shaking his head. "We're not going to make it," he said in a tired voice. "We're going to miss the opening of the exhibition."

His friends looked shocked. "Why?" Joe asked. "You told me you guys were right on target two days ago!"

"That was two days ago," David replied, sounding grim. "That was before we got hit with this."

He pointed toward a glowing monitor. Instead of showing landscapes or animated dinosaurs, all the screen had on it was a shimmering blue field and a blinking white dash.

Sam said, "Uh . . . there's nothing there, David."

David waved his hands in frustration. "Oh, our program's *there,* all right. We just can't get to it. Someone slipped a computer virus into our system."

"A virus?" Sam asked. "Uh-oh."

"A really nasty one," David told them. "It eats the boot sectors, which help identify data. It doesn't do anything to the actual data—except make sure we can't get to any of it. Once the boot sectors are gone, the data may as well be on Mars, for all the good it does us."

Wishbone looked up at David's frustrated face. The normally cheerful David wore a miserable expression. Wishbone put his paw on David's knee. "Cheer up, David. It can't be as bad as all that." David reached down and absently scratched the dog's ears.

"Is it all gone?" Joe said, bending over the monitor.

"Oh, not all of it—we were lucky, I guess. We caught on to the virus soon enough to save most of the programs, but it's drop-kicked all our schedules right out the window. We're going to need days to rebuild everything. It'll probably be tomorrow or the day after before we're even sure what we saved. The virus may have destroyed data that we need for the program."

"How did the virus get into the system?" Joe wondered. "Don't you have protection programs to guard against this kind of thing?"

"We've got the best that money can buy," Maddy Kingston said. She pushed back in her chair and ran her fingers through her messy hair. "But whoever hit us was very clever and first took the virus sensors off-line. The culprit must have a thorough knowledge of computers. It was a very difficult job to get past all of our security measures and load the virus directly into the system."

"Was it hidden in something you downloaded off the Internet?" Sam asked.

"No way," Maddy replied, sipping coffee from a mug with a picture of a computer on it. "None of these machines can get to the Net. It's all part of Ben's tight security procedures. No outside downloading, no possible break of security. The virus didn't sneak in that way. Someone corrupted one of the disks, and we fed it in manually."

"That's the really awful thing," David said, looking very discouraged. "Everyone who works back here or comes back here and touches anything has to have special clearance." David sighed. "What if the vandal isn't breaking in from the outside? What if he's already *here?*" David continued. "What if he's one of *us?*"

Double whoa! Wishbone thought, his ears standing straight up. *No wonder everyone's nervous!* Alertly, he scanned the crowded room. Wishbone could see the way all the technicians kept glancing around nervously. He noticed the way they held their bodies so that they covered their keyboards and screens in an effort not to let anyone see what they were doing.

The mysterious vandal scores in a big way! How can all

of these people hope to work together if they can't trust one another anymore? This is terrible!

"Do you know anything about this person?" Joe asked. "Do you have any clues?"

Maddy said, "Oh, we've got a clue, all right—we know he's really proud of himself and really good at what he does. Show them, David," she told him, pointing to her computer.

Wishbone watched with great interest as David moved to his keyboard and carefully typed a word.

"Bonedig?" asked Joe, reading over David's shoulder.

David nodded. "Whoever did this has a really sick sense of humor."

David hit Enter, and the skeleton of a Tyrannosaurus appeared on the screen. It stood there for a second, then shattered into pieces. It was immediately replaced by another skeleton that also crumbled apart. Over and over, the dinosaurs appeared; over and over, they fell apart—until the bottom of the screen was littered with nothing but splinters of digital bones.

Broken bones! What a waste! David sure is right—whoever this guy is, he's got a really sick sense of humor!

Chapter Seven

The next Saturday morning, Wishbone sat beside Joe, in the very first row. He wagged his tail happily. "Great seats, Joe! From here we can see everything. I'm glad David got us V.I.P. treatment—you're a Very Important Person, and I'm a Very Important Pup!"

Joe sat on the aisle side in the first row of folding chairs that had been set up inside the main exhibition hall of the museum. Next to him was Sam, and next to her was David. All three kids were excited and talkative. David was especially happy to see this moment come, since he had worked hard to repair the damage done by the computer vandal. In front of them stood the dinosaur exhibit, although all the skeletons were still hidden from view by dropcloths until the grand unveiling. A reading stand had been set up in front of them, with a pitcher of water, some glasses, and a microphone.

Around the four friends, including Wishbone, were nearly a hundred other people, including college professors, students of all ages, people from the press, and some Oakdale town officials. Everyone was murmuring and pointing, wondering what lay behind the cloths. Far over on the right, Wanda Gilmore sat with her camera ready, and a yellow legal pad was open on her lap. Wishbone thought she seemed determined not to lose any chance of reporting on the latest dinosaur news.

Wishbone smelled Dr. Breckenridge, and he looked over his shoulder. "Hi, Doc! Thanks for the invitation."

Dressed in freshly pressed khakis and a sun helmet, Dr. Breckenridge was making his way toward the reading stand set up in front of the exhibit. He paused and leaned over to speak to David, removing his hat as he did so. "Well, David, I want to thank you again for all your hard work on the interactive exhibit."

David smiled at the paleontologist and said seriously, "Thanks, Dr. Breckenridge. I'm sorry that the full animations aren't ready yet."

"They'll come along in time," the fossil hunter assured him. "What happened wasn't your fault. A scientist has to keep plugging away, even when everything seems to go wrong."

With a nod, David replied, "Sure. You didn't give up when it took you five years to make your great discoveries. I won't let a few setbacks upset me."

Dr. Breckenridge ran his hand over his pulled-back blond hair, and his ponytail bobbed. "Yes," Dr. Breckenridge said, nodding. "That's the only attitude to have, David. In science, you just have to keep trying and trying. Excuse me now."

He made his way to the front and shook hands with Margaret Bradbury, the Windom Foundation representative. They whispered to each other for a few seconds. Then Dr. Breckenridge stepped up to the stand. Wishbone thought the man's expression was very serious—almost gloomy. The scientist took his glasses off, polished them against his shirt, and then cleared his throat. The murmur of voices from the audience dropped.

"Thank you," Dr. Breckenridge said in his shy, soft voice. "It's my pleasure today to present to you some of the fossils we uncovered on our digs. First, we have a complete skeleton of a young Camarasaurus. As you will see, even a half-grown Camarasaurus was still pretty big!"

He turned and gestured, and an electric engine whined. One of the dropcloths flew upward, uncovering a long-necked, long-tailed dinosaur skeleton. It was about twenty-eight feet from its nose to the tip of its tail. The animal had been assembled as if it were taking a step forward—its neck curved as it looked to the left, and its left front leg lifted.

Whoa! thought Wishbone. *Would you look at the size of those leg bones!*

One by one, Dr. Breckenridge revealed the other skeletons. Next was an Allosaurus. At sixteen feet in height, it was a somewhat smaller cousin of the *T. rex*. Then he unveiled two seagoing lizards, an Icthyosaur and a Mosaosaur, both of them larger than a porpoise. The next skeleton he brought into view was a truck-sized, three-horned Triceratops. After that came a twenty-foot-tall strange duckbill dinosaur with a huge curving bony crest on its head, Parasaurolophus. Wishbone liked them all. He wagged his tail with appreciation.

Then Dr. Breckenridge hesitated for several seconds. Only one dropcloth remained draped over a large exhibit directly behind him. He turned and looked at the hidden shapes. Then he looked back at the audience and smiled tightly. "And last, but I certainly hope not least, I am about to present to you our most amazing discovery."

He looked down at his notes and shuffled a stack of papers. Wishbone leaned forward. "Come on, Doc! Don't keep us in suspense! Show us the bones! Show us the bones!"

In a voice even softer than usual, Dr. Breckenridge murmured, "I'm not a very good speaker, I'm afraid. I'm more used to digging up bones and writing about them than talking to a room full of people. Please forgive me if I seem a little nervous. The Windom Foundation has been very generous to me. When it first sponsored this particular expedition I had planned—the first American expedition to explore four separate fossil sites at the same time—the foundation promised me financial backing for one year. Fortunately, at the end of that year, I was able to report some . . . uh . . . some remarkable fossils finds. As a result, the foundation extended its support for two years, and then for an additional two. I am very grateful. We made many fascinating finds. Some are here, and others are still being studied."

The electric motor whined again. Wishbone thought the sound startled Dr. Breckenridge. He turned and stared as the last dropcloth soared upward. The crowd gasped. Wishbone heard oohs and ahhs all around him. He could understand. This exhibit *was* different from all the others. "Three dinosaurs! And they look *dangerous!*"

Wishbone and the others stared at three slim, long-legged predators. They stood on their hind legs and were in a position as if running forward, their small front limbs clutching like claws. The skeletons were a shiny brownish-orange, and their razor-sharp teeth gleamed. They weren't giants. In fact, they were only about as tall as Joe. But with their bared teeth and long, sharp claws, they looked fierce.

"A . . . a new species of dinosaur." Dr. Breckenridge paused. "I . . . uh . . . have named this species Mundioraptor. The name . . . uh . . . means 'elegant thief.' All

my life I've believed that during the two hundred million years when dinosaurs walked the earth, there was more than enough opportunity for them to develop intelligence. In fact, I have always believed that was bound to happen."

Cameras were flashing like crazy. Wishbone saw Wanda stand up on her chair and snap several pictures. Then she called out, "Dr. Breckenridge, do you mean these were *intelligent* dinosaurs?"

Dr. Breckenridge paused for a moment to take a drink of water. "I wouldn't say these were as intelligent as a modern human," he said. "But they have a larger skull than any other dinosaur of their size—about seventy percent larger, in fact. That indicates a bigger brain. Notice the forelimbs, too. A *T. rex* has only two fingers on each forelimb, but these creatures have three. And one of them is a thumb."

"What does that mean?" asked an eager woman in the audience. Wishbone recognized the speaker as Alice Zane, from the Zenith *Times* newspaper. But from where he sat, he couldn't see her.

Dr. Breckenridge stammered again, "W-well, the limbs are more muscular and developed than on other predators of this type. A thumb means they could g-grasp objects. Bones, for example, or sticks, or rocks—"

"They used *tools?*" Alice Zane demanded.

Dr. Breckenridge blinked. "Well, they may have," he almost whispered. "They may even have developed some kind of a language and a primitive society."

"Is that why someone is trying to destroy the exhibit?" the reporter pressed on. "Are they a little too human-like for comfort?"

Everyone started to talk at once. Dr. Breckenridge frowned and held his hands up for silence. "I—I think I've said enough. I'll let Mr. Benjamin McIntyre respond to your . . . uh . . . questions about security. Thank you." He sat down.

Ben McIntyre looked surprised, but he stepped up to the stand. In his deep voice, he said, "The person who's threatened the exhibit is probably someone who is mentally unstable. Anyway, no one is going to destroy this exhibit. I have a top-notch security team here, and special guard dogs are on duty. No one will get past us." He paused, then added in a strong voice, "No one!"

As soon as the presentation was over, David glanced at Joe and Sam. He had a hard time hiding his enthusiasm. "Want to see the interactive exhibit?" he asked them, trying to sound casual. "It's a lot more complete now."

Joe nodded. "I'd like to get a closer look at the skeletons, but I don't think we could fight through the crowd. And Wishbone might get stepped on."

"Come on," Sam said. "We can see the skeletons later. I want to see David's animations!"

Joe, Sam, David, and Wishbone made their way over to one of the computer monitors that stood in alcoves around the exhibits. "It won't be much," David warned, though he was trying to hide a grin. "I still have a lot of work to do."

"It'll be fine," Joe said. He looked at the screen, which showed a shifting pattern of colors. In the center, a panel read: TOUCH HERE TO BEGIN. Joe touched the screen.

A map of the western United States appeared. From an overhead speaker a voice said, "Welcome to the great fossil-hunting area of North America. We'll go on a dig today. Touch the screen and select a site."

David's grin spread from ear to ear. "That's Dr. Breckenridge's voice," he said. "He's been great! He agreed to record the script, and he let me help write it. All right, guys, try it out."

"Where do you want to dig?" Joe asked Sam.

"Hmm . . . right here," Sam said, leaning forward to put her finger on Montana.

David looked on with pride as the screen changed. It showed a landscape of grassy, rolling hills. A river ran through them. The grass waved in a gentle breeze, and white clouds drifted in the blue sky. "This is the way your site looked during the last part of the Cretaceous period, some seventy million years ago. Let's see how the area has altered over time."

"Cool," Joe said, as the picture shimmered and rearranged itself.

The monitor next showed a dry, barren land, with

rocky hills and cliffs. "This is the area today," the voice told them. "Now it's time to dig."

Joe selected a spot and touched it. The cross-section showed that no dinosaur bones lay under his choice. "Don't be disappointed," the voice said calmly. "Fossilization happens only rarely. Try again."

"Want a hint?" David asked, watching as Joe hesitated. "I'd go for something where the ground has eroded a little."

This time Joe chose the base of a cliff. "All right!" he said, as the cutaway shot showed a jumble of bones. "Let's move them up." He began to touch and drag the bones to the surface. Soon he unearthed a huge skull with sharp teeth in it.

The computerized voice said, "Now you can begin to make some observations. What kind of dinosaur do you think this is?" The choices appeared on the right side of the screen: plant-eating land dinosaur; meat-eating land dinosaur; flying reptile; swimming reptile.

"Gotta be a meat-eater," Joe said. "Look at those teeth!" He touched his answer.

"You're right," the voice said. "The rows of sharp teeth and the strong jaws show that this is a Carnosaurus, or meat-eating land dinosaur. See if you can assemble the skeleton."

David watched with pleasure as Joe and Sam touched and dragged the bones. It was like piecing together a jigsaw puzzle. When they had finished, David sighed and said, "I'm sorry it's not completely finished, guys."

"This is fantastic!" Joe said. "David, there's nothing wrong with this."

"Well, I wanted it to be better," David said. Then, allowing a hint of pride to come through in his voice, he asked, "You really like it?"

"Everyone's going to love it," Sam insisted. "Hey! Look at this—here are the front legs!"

"And two fingers!" Joe said. "That means it's a *T. rex!*"

Sure enough, when the computer prompted them to decide what species the dinosaur was, it turned out to be a *Tyrannosaurus rex*. The computer explained that the name meant "the tyrant king of the dinosaurs." It went on to point out what a fierce predator the beast must have been. Then the picture changed, and the assembled skeleton stalked the grassy plains of Cretaceous Montana. After that, the program ended.

"Great!" Joe said. "David, I think this is the neatest thing you've ever done."

"I agree," said someone behind him. He turned. Dr. Maddy Kingston stood there, a big smile on her face. "David's done a wonderful job."

Joe saw that Dr. Breckenridge and Ms. Bradbury were headed their way. "I thought the computer presentation wasn't ready," Ms. Bradbury said.

"It isn't complete yet," Maddy answered, "but it's running. We still have some fine-tuning to do."

With a little sigh, Ms. Bradbury said, "I do hope it will be complete very soon. As soon as possible. It's very costly to prepare."

Dr. Breckenridge put his hand on David's shoulder. "The computer team's doing fine work," he said firmly. "In fact, I have the feeling that when people leave the exhibit, they're not going to be raving over the fossils. They'll remember David's virtual dinosaur hunt best of all."

David glowed. He smiled at Dr. Breckenridge and nodded his thanks.

Ms. Bradbury nodded. "That's very good. Monday will be a big day for us, though. Will your computers be ready by then, Dr. Kingston?"

Maddy said, "With hard work—maybe. We've got all the specimens programmed except for the new one, the Mundioraptor. A computer virus wiped that part out completely. We have to double-check everything to make sure the virus isn't still in hiding. We want everything to function without glitches, so we need time to rewrite and retest the programs."

"There goes the rest of the weekend," David said to Joe and Sam in a whisper, as the adults walked toward the Triceratops exhibit.

Joe, Wishbone, Sam, and David moved away from the computer and into the exhibit area. "Will you be able to do it?" Sam asked David.

David calculated, wondered, then shrugged. "Who knows? It means hours at the keyboard. And there are always bugs to chase down. It's fun in a way, but it's a lot of hard work, too."

"Can we help?" Joe asked.

David shook his head. "Can you run a CAD program and animate it?"

"No. Sorry," Joe told him. "If there's anything else—"

"I know one thing," Sam said. "I'll talk my dad into supplying you and the other programmers with pizza. How's that?"

"That's a help," David said, thinking of how hungry the computer team always seemed to be. "I know everyone would appreciate that!"

Wishbone barked.

Joe laughed. "I think Wishbone just volunteered to help get rid of any leftover pizza!"

Chapter Eight

That evening, Joe boxed up another extra-large pizza, checked off the toppings—cheese, Italian sausage, pepperoni, olives, and peppers—on the top of the box, and added it to his stack. He noticed that Sam was one pizza ahead of him. "The next one's mine," he said. "You've boxed several already. How do you go so fast?"

"I've had practice," Sam reminded him with a smile. She slipped three boxed pizzas into a large insulated pouch. "Programmers can sure eat a lot of pizza," she said, grinning.

Joe heard Wishbone scratching at the door. "Be patient, buddy," he called. "The health department won't let you come into the kitchen. We'll be out in a minute."

Walter Kepler scooped the last pizza from the oven with a smooth, practiced motion. Then he laid it into one of the flattened boxes. "Here you are, Joe," he said. "This one is the Honolulu Special—ham, mild peppers, and pineapple."

Joe folded the box into shape, sliced the pizza, shut the box, and checked off the ingredients. "Thanks a lot, Mr. Kepler," he said. "I know the programmers will appreciate these."

"My compliments to them," Mr. Kepler replied with a smile. "Just tell Dr. Breckenridge that all I ask in return is for Pepper Pete's pizza to be named the Official Pizza of the Dinosaur Exhibit." He turned back to the oven and said, "I have some leftover hamburger here that I won't need. Think Wishbone might enjoy it?"

"He always does," Joe said with a grin. He took the hamburger outside on a paper plate, and Wishbone made short work of it. The kitchen door swung open, and Joe turned to see Sam coming out with six pizzas. It looked like quite a load.

"Sorry I can't drive you out to the museum," Mr. Kepler said from behind her. "But I have to keep the restaurant open. Will you be all right?"

"Sure," Joe said. "It isn't that far." He took three pizzas from Sam. Even through the insulated bags, they felt warm. "Ready?"

"Let's go," Sam said with a grin.

It was a fifteen-minute walk to the college campus, but the evening was mild and clear. They arrived at the museum and went to the side entrance, where Joe pressed an elbow against the security buzzer. After a moment, a guard unlocked the door. "Hi," he said. "Dinner for the computer crew, huh?"

"Come down and have some," Sam said. "We have plenty."

The guard chuckled. "Thanks, but maybe I'll wait until it's time for my break. Mr. McIntyre wouldn't like it if I left my post." He closed and locked the door. Then he pressed a button that summoned the freight elevator. "Have a good evening."

The elevator doors clanked open, and Joe turned to the guard and said, "You, too." Then Joe said, "Where are you, Wishbone?"

"He's right behind you," Sam said, stepping into the elevator. "Come on, Wishbone!"

They rode down to the basement. The programmers gave Joe and Sam a cheer as they stepped into the computer room. Joe saw that Dr. Breckenridge was there, talking to David. The two of them waved as Maddy came over.

"Wonderful!" Maddy said. "Sam, be sure to thank your dad for us. Now, we want to keep the food away from the computers, so let's put these on the table against the wall. We'll let everyone help themselves."

A dozen programmers descended on the pizza boxes, and slices started to go fast. David and Dr. Breckenridge came over, and Joe said, "Have some pizza, Dr. Breckenridge?"

The scientist smiled. "Thanks, Joe." He took a slice and added, "David tells me that you used to be a real dinosaur buff."

"I still am, I guess," Joe said, feeling a little shy. "I've got some of your books—I mean, not the technical ones you wrote for other paleontologists, but ones like *Dinosaur Diary* and *Dinosaur Hunter*. That one's my favorite. I must have read it a million times. I've been wondering if you'd autograph the books for me."

"Sure," Dr. Breckenridge replied. "Do you know why I wrote those books?"

Joe just shrugged his shoulders.

"Because that's how I got interested in dinosaurs when I was even younger than you," the professional fossil hunter replied. "I read some of Roy Chapman Andrews's wonderful books about hunting for dinosaur fossils in the Gobi Desert in Mongolia. After that, I was hooked. I *had* to get into this field of work."

"Sort of the way I feel about computers," David said.

Dr. Breckenridge clapped his hand on David's arm.

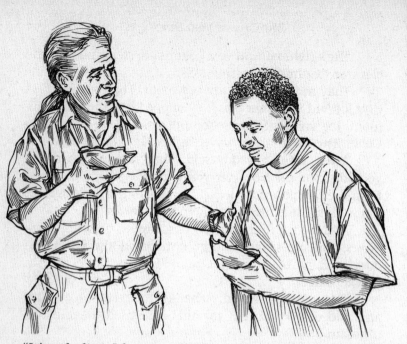

"It's a feeling I know well," he said. "I fell in love with dinosaurs when I was six years old, and here I am still chasing them. And if there is anything I have learned, it's that you don't give up when there are little setbacks. Always remember that. I've got to run along now. So long, everyone, and keep up the good work."

There followed a round of good-byes, partly muffled by mouths eating bites of pizza. Then Dr. Breckenridge was gone. Sam, David, and Joe got some pizza for themselves and found a quiet corner. Joe saw that Wishbone was using his expert doggie begging skills. He was already running up a good score in a game of Hi There, Please Give Me Your Crust.

For twenty minutes David talked about the progress he was making with the interactive display. Using the notes Maddy had given him, he was using his computer to create the individual bones of a Mundioraptor skeleton.

Sam yawned. "I brought my book," she said. "I think I'll read one of the stories." She pulled the paperback out of her jacket pocket.

"What story are you reading now?" Joe asked.

"It's called 'Silver Blaze,'" Sam said. "It's about a racehorse—"

"Oh, right," Joe said. "In that one, Silver Blaze is a famous racehorse. He disappears, and his trainer, John Straker, is murdered that same night. Colonel Ross, the horse's owner, asks Sherlock Holmes to—"

"All right," Sam said with a laugh. "I know *you've* read the story. Now let me read it, and don't tell me the end— Oh!"

Joe jumped when, suddenly, the museum's lights all went out at once. The computer room was immediately plunged into complete darkness. Then Joe heard some loud *clacks* from the direction of the door.

"Power failure!" someone yelled. "Has everybody saved their programs?"

A couple of people groaned. "I probably lost the last five or six minutes," a woman's voice said.

A boy answered her. "I turned off the automatic backup on my machine because it kept interrupting me. I think I lost half an hour."

"I'm glad I backed up my files," David said. "It's really dark in here, isn't it?"

"I can't see *anything*," Sam answered.

Joe felt Wishbone press against his leg. He reached down and patted the Jack Russell terrier reassuringly. "It's okay, buddy. I'll take you outside—"

"You can't," David told him from the darkness. "If the power goes off, the exit doors automatically lock."

"You mean we're trapped here?" Sam asked calmly.

Across the room, someone turned on a flashlight.

"Everyone all right?" asked Maddy, as she held their only light source. "I don't know why the battery-powered emergency lights haven't come on. Bill, is that you? Climb on the chair and check the emergency light over the door."

A tall, skinny young man did as Maddy asked. "The switch is off," he said. Then he clicked something. Two lights flicked on. They rested atop a square gray metal box over the door. Joe blinked. Everything looked different in the pale yellow glow of the eerie lights. Different and a little weird.

"I'll call for help," Maddy told them. She went to her terminal and then picked up the telephone receiver. After a moment, she put it down again. "Great. The phones are dead."

Everyone began to murmur. "I'll bet it's the vandal," David said. "He's trapped us down here for some reason. We need to let Security know."

Joe stared at the battery-powered lights. Next to them was an air vent, covered with an aluminum grille. It was just big enough for Wishbone to get through. "Maybe we can send for help," he said. "At least I think we can get someone's attention. Come here, Wishbone!"

Joe picked Wishbone up. Then he, Sam, and David went over to Maddy.

"I'm sorry you kids are trapped here," Maddy told them. "At midnight, a security man will come by—"

"We might be able to get help sooner than that," Joe said. "If we could just get into that air vent above the door—"

Maddy looked up. "It's too small," she said.

"Not for Wishbone," Joe replied.

Maddy's eyebrows shot up. "I see what you mean. Do you think he could do it?"

Wishbone squirmed in Joe's arms. "I think that he's itching to do it!" Joe said.

Bill climbed up on the chair again and found that the grille opened on a hinge. He swung it open, and Joe handed Wishbone up. "Go get help, buddy!" Joe said urgently. "Let someone know we're here!"

Bill boosted Wishbone up. The dog scrambled into the dark opening, and Joe heard his nails scrabbling on aluminum.

"Do you think he understands?" David asked.

"I hope so," Joe said. "Get help, boy! Get help!"

Wishbone heard Joe call, "Get help, boy! Get help!" He crept forward on his tummy, feeling excited.

"Spy stuff! All right, Joe, Agent Double-Oh-Dog is on the case! Here I go!"

Within a few feet, Wishbone was plunged into darkness, but he used his nose as a guide. His senses of smell and hearing were so sharp that, even without light, he got a clear mental picture of his surroundings.

"Let me see . . . I'm about ten feet in. A ventilation pipe leads off to the left, but the room there is dark. It's a dead end. So I'll go past that, then turn right at the next bend."

Wishbone quickly became aware of one thing. Creeping through air ducts wasn't nearly as glamourous in real life as it seemed to be in the movies.

In the movies, he thought, *all the air-conditioning ducts are clean and shiny. This one has about ten years of dust collected in it, though! Ah—ahh——AAHH-CHOOO!*

A faint red light glimmered ahead. Wishbone crawled to another vent and peered through. A red Exit sign glowed in the darkness. *Hmm,* he thought, *that means the lights aren't off all over the museum. Which means that the security people won't have any reason to think something's wrong in the computer lab.* He crawled past the vent and saw a brighter light ahead. He could also smell something. He took a deep sniff to be sure. *Dobermans! The Marx brothers are close by!*

Wishbone scrambled forward, slipping several times on the slick aluminum. Then he came to another vent and peered outside, down into a lighted room. It looked like a storage room—at least, lots of big cardboard boxes were stacked around. Pacing around on the floor were four large dogs.

Wishbone barked, and their heads came around sharply. They barked back at him, probably wondering how Wishbone had managed to get all the way up there to the ceiling. Wishbone thought they looked lost. Then, watching them, Wishbone realized that something wasn't right. The dogs shouldn't be shut up in a storage room—they were supposed to be on patrol!

He gave them one last look. "I think I understand—somebody has locked you guys in! Don't worry! Agent Double-Oh-Dog will bring help! Hang on, guys!

One last vent, and this time Wishbone looked out onto a staircase. A dim light burned there, and Wishbone caught a clear whiff of outside air. He realized that somewhere a door was open—one that should have been locked at this time of night. He put his head against the grille and shoved. He felt it give a little, so he pushed harder. Then, with a clatter, the vent flew open.

Wishbone put his head out the opening. It was a long way down. Since the stairwell was only about eight feet wide, however, if he could jump across it, he would land on the stairs going up. Wishbone judged the distance. He backed up a little, tensed, then made the leap!

Oof! He caught the edge of the step with his front paws. Then he raced upstairs. Sure enough, the door at the top was open a crack, and he squeezed through and was outside the museum.

Like a flash, Wishbone ran around to the front of the building and up the front steps. He could see a security guard sitting at the desk inside, reading a magazine. Wishbone began to bark frantically and to scratch at the door.

"Hey! Could you give me a little help here? My friends are in trouble! Over here!"

The security officer looked up, his expression one of surprise. He made a shooing gesture.

Wishbone barked even louder. "Hurry! Come on! Over here!"

Shaking his head, the man got up and came to the door. He unlocked it and opened it a crack. "Go away, pup. We're closed— Hey!"

Wishbone squeezed inside and ran down the hall,

barking at the top of his lungs. Behind him he heard the guard's running footsteps approaching.

Then someone stepped out in front of him. "Jackson, what's going on?"

Wishbone recognized the voice of Ben McIntyre, the head of security. The brave Jack Russell terrier ran past the man, toward the elevators. "Follow me! Agent Double-Oh-Dog to the rescue! Gangwayyyyy!"

"That's Joe Talbot's dog," McIntyre said. "Come on!"

Wishbone waited by the elevators. The two guards hurried up behind him.

McIntyre pressed the Down button with his thumb. "Something's up," he said. "We'd better check it out."

Wishbone rode down with them. When the doors opened at the basement level, Wishbone raced ahead, leading the security officers to the computer lab.

Jackson said, "It's dark in this wing."

"The power is off," McIntyre responded. "Here—I can unlock the doors manually."

Wishbone heard the jingle of keys. A moment later, the lab door swung open, to sounds of relief from the trapped programmers.

"He did it!" someone yelled. "The little dog saved us!"

Wishbone struck a proud pose. "Was there ever any doubt? And we double-oh agents are *not* little, thank you very much. We're carefully chosen to be just the right height . . . . Wow!"

The lights had just come on, blinding him. Wishbone shut his eyes. He wished he could shut his ears. . . .

Because all at once every alarm in the museum began to ring, buzz, or shriek.

Chapter Nine

David was in the lead with Wishbone as a thundering crowd of security guards and programmers rushed down the marble hall of the museum toward the exhibit hall. *Something's happened,* David thought desperately. *Something awful has happened!*

The hall seemed to stretch on forever, although he knew it couldn't be more than a hundred feet long. Behind him, he could hear Ben McIntyre barking out orders and Maddy Kingston gasping, asking questions as she tried to keep up.

Then they all burst into the central exhibit hall and staggered to a dead stop. No one said a word as they all stared in horror at the sight before them.

"Oh, no!" David groaned, breaking the silence.

"What is it?" Sam cried, as she and Joe caught up with him. Then she saw what her friend was looking at, and her eyes grew wide. "Oh, the poor things!"

David could only nod silently. Slowly, they all moved forward past the striding Allosaurus and the lumbering Camarosaurus skeletons to where the Mundioraptors had been posed on their platform.

David swallowed a hard lump in his throat as he stared at what had happened.

The magnificent exhibit had been completely destroyed. The elegant skeletons were smashed to pieces and scattered all over the floor. Whoever had done it hadn't been satisfied with just knocking over all of the dinosaurs. Many of the individual bones had been pounded to pieces. At least one of the great grinning skulls had been split, then split again.

David turned away. He couldn't help but think how upset Dr. Breckenridge was going to be. Setbacks were one thing, but this was a disaster. His chest felt tight, and his eyes stung.

"Harpo, Groucho, Chico, Zeppo!" Ben McIntyre boomed. His angry voice echoed through the exhibit hall. "Where are you clowns!" He was immediately answered by a loud chorus of barking from down in one of the stairwells.

"They're in storage room seven, Ben," the security guard named Johnston called as he came running down the hall. "I can hear them barking, but somebody locked them in and then sabotaged the lock."

Ben shoved Johnston aside and ran down a flight of stairs. David and Joe followed close behind. When Mr. McIntyre finally reached the storage room door, he glared through the little glass window set into it.

Over his shoulder, David was able to spot first one slim canine head, then another, as the Dobermans leaped up to try to see their master. Ben fumbled with a large ring of keys. He tried several, then snarled, "Someone's broken off a piece of metal inside the lock—a paper clip or something. Stand back!" With a mighty kick, he broke the door open.

Joe gasped. "Sir, won't the museum have to repair—"

"They can bill me if necessary," Ben shot back. The slim black-and-brown dogs scrambled through the shattered door. He snapped his fingers loudly and the four froze, their sharp eyes hard on his face. Ben knelt down and stared back at them. "Go. Find. Now," he whispered.

The Dobermans exploded past David, nearly bowling him over as they charged fiercely upstairs. He, Joe, and Mr. McIntyre ran up close behind them. They saw the Dobermans sweep past the startled crowd in the hallway, then speed back toward the exhibit hall.

As they rushed along, the sound of loud barking drifted up to meet them.

"Wishbone!" Joe said in amazement. "Hey, that's Wishbone!"

The Marx brothers hesitated for the merest second, then bounded off in the direction of the barking.

"They have the scent already," Ben McIntyre rumbled, striding forward. "Good boys—that's my good boys." He shouted, "Johnston! You call the police! I want them here *yesterday!*"

"Yes, sir!"

"Did you see the look on his face?" Sam whispered, sounding frightened. David had seen the look, all right. He knew that McIntyre was furious. Under that anger, though, was another feeling—one as sad as his own.

Then they were on the far side of the remains of the dinosaur exhibit. Wishbone was there, still barking. The four Dobermans were stalking in a tight circle around a figure that lay crumpled on the hard marble floor, not moving at all.

"Sit! Stay!" McIntyre bellowed. The Marx brothers obediently settled down onto their haunches. Even Wishbone obeyed, sitting right beside David's foot.

The big man slipped silently into the circle of dogs

and knelt down next to the huddled figure on the floor. Carefully, he turned it over so the face became visible. The humorless smile on his face grew even colder.

"Well, well, what a surprise," he said.

David stared in amazement at the unconscious form of Alice Zane, sprawled there on the floor. And he gasped when he suddenly saw the large sledgehammer that lay next to her.

Wishbone gave the four Dobermans a look full of praise. "Good work, guys—you really catch on fast! Come on! She may have an accomplice!" He turned and sped toward the front doors. When he realized the other canines weren't following, Wishbone turned and barked once. "Well, come on—the humans can handle it from here! Double-Oh-Dog to the rescue!" Wishbone realized then what was wrong with the four Dobermans. They never did anything on their own! He barked again to get their attention. "Come on! Last chance! Act like dogs, not mice!"

As silent as could be, Harpo, Groucho, Chico, and Zeppo came after him, their long legs ghosting across the marble floors. Behind them, Wishbone could hear Ben McIntyre giving orders; people hurried to obey them.

He'll be all right, Wishbone thought. *I'm sure he can take care of the suspect. But for really top-notch chasing and tracking, you just gotta have a dog—or even five dogs!*

Wishbone couldn't shove the heavy double doors of the museum open. But when the Dobermans saw what he was trying to do, they all stood on their hind legs and put their combined weight on the doors. They swung open slowly.

A second later, Wishbone and his furious followers streaked out the doorway of the museum and onto the campus of Oakdale College. It was night, and the full moon cast shadows like clutching claws from the trees that surrounded the courtyard. Even the friendly old oak in the center of that green open space looked somehow threatening.

Wishbone's mind was racing. *We gotta be alert! Who knows who or what might be hiding around here. Stick with me, guys, and we'll have this wrapped up before morning!*

The dogs searched around the campus. Wishbone was always in the lead, with the Marx brothers tailing his every move. *So this is what it's like to be a wolf-pack leader,* the Jack Russell terrier thought as they stalked. *Loping along under the full moon, my trusty pack following my every move. Cool!*

Finally, they came to a flowerbed, which had been seriously dug up.

"Whoa!" Wishbone came to a stop so suddenly that Harpo, Groucho, Chico, and Zeppo nearly plowed into one another.

Four pairs of alert eyes zeroed in on him as he paced back and forth through the tilled soil, his nose working overtime.

"Yeah, yeah—this is interesting! This is what we're looking for!"

Wishbone began to dig. The dirt was loose, and it showered away behind him as he frantically scraped away at it with his nails. The fine soil bounced off the solid chests of the Marx brothers as they watched.

Wishbone paused and looked over his shoulder. "What are you guys waiting for? Come on! Dig, guys, dig! Trust me, it's a lot of fun—have I ever led you wrong before?"

Harpo looked at Groucho, who looked at Chico, who looked at Zeppo. Then, almost as one, the four lean but powerful Dobermans were next to Wishbone, ripping into the ground with their sharp nails. In a matter of moments, the first long gray shape came into view.

Wishbone sniffed it and barked for joy. *"Eureka! We've struck pay dirt—so to speak. Teamwork does the trick every time! Now, if we can just get these home!"*

The Dobermans continued to dig. Over the noise they made, Wishbone heard another sound. His head jerked up, the fur on his neck bristling. *Somebody's out there, trying to keep quiet!*

Wishbone couldn't risk barking to alert the others. Carefully, he looked around. The shadows near the museum seemed to be even darker, as if someone had drawn them in with black ink.

Wishbone focused all his sharp instincts. *There, in the shadow of that oak tree—is that . . . a dinosaur? It sure looks like a dinosaur. A very small one, perhaps . . .* If only the wind were blowing right, Wishbone could have smelled it. Unfortunately, the object was downwind. A four-foot-tall figure with a long tail and a huge head. It waved its forearms. . . .

Then Harpo bumped into Wishbone, distracting him as the Doberman hauled one of the long shapes out of the ground. Then when Wishbone looked back, the dinosaur, or whatever it had been, was gone, vanished into the thick of the night.

Feeling helpless as he waited to give his statement to the police, Joe stood a few feet away from three adults who were arguing.

"I tell you, I had absolutely nothing to do with this!"

Alice Zane sat huddled between Ben McIntyre and Officer Krulla, from the Oakdale Police Department. The young woman looked totally miserable.

"I find that very hard to believe, Ms. Zane," Ben McIntyre said in an accusing voice.

"Please, Mr. McIntyre," Officer Krulla said patiently, as his gazed shifted from Alice to Ben. "I'll handle this." He held up a clear plastic bag that contained a crumpled piece of cloth. "We'll have to have this tested, but I think it's been soaked with chloroform, all right. If that's the case, it's strong enough to put anyone to sleep, so maybe Ms. Zane is not the vandal."

Ben snorted and stood there, his arms crossed over his massive chest. Officer Krulla sighed and turned back to Alice.

"All right, ma'am, let's go through your story one more time, shall we?" the police officer said.

Joe looked over his shoulder. People were still milling around the rotunda. It seemed that none of the programmers and other museum staffers wanted to leave the scene. They stood huddled in little groups, talking in hushed voices.

Joe had called his mom. Even though it was late, the kids couldn't leave until Officer Krulla interviewed Joe, David, and Sam. Later, as Joe caught sight of his mom, who was talking to Wanda over in front of the sabotaged dinosaur exhibit, he saw someone else coming down the hall. "It's Dr. Breckenridge," he said quietly.

David turned to look. Dr. Breckenridge walked into the exhibit hall and stopped, his eyes wide. He staggered and put a hand against the wall. Joe shuddered, reading the pain on the scientist's face. Then he shook his head and came forward, his face becoming a mask of anger.

"Why?" Dr. Breckenridge boomed. His voice was not at all soft now, but harsh and full of pain. "Why would *anyone* do this?"

Several of the museum employees clustered around him. He ignored them and pushed past them to pick up one of the Mundioraptor skulls. It had been shattered. He held the fragments in his hands as if he were cradling a fallen child. He stood there and shook his head over the remains. He looked absolutely miserable.

"I want to talk to him," David whispered. "He's pretty upset."

And so are you, Joe thought, looking sympathetically at his good friend. He watched David make his way over to the scientist. Dr. Breckenridge showed the broken bones to David and shook his head again. David touched his arm and said something to him. Joe thought both of them looked totally heartbroken. Joe turned away, facing Alice and Officer Krulla.

"Listen, how many times do I have to say this?" Alice asked wearily. "Yes, I'll admit that I stayed behind after the museum closed. Yes, I'll admit that I hid here in the exhibit. Yes, I'll admit that it was a stupid thing to do, but I was following a lead!"

"And what lead was that, Ms. Zane?" Officer Krulla said, chewing the end of his pencil.

"I can't tell you my source," Alice said with a sigh. "I had reason to believe someone might show up to damage the fossils. So I hid out here. All I got to show for it was a face full of chloroform. And that's all I know. Honest."

"You want to tell me how you got past my dogs?" Ben McIntyre interrupted.

Alice glared at him. "I got past the dogs because there *weren't* any. This place was empty and as quiet as a tomb . . . and just as cold." She rubbed her arms.

Mr. McIntyre's face turned red. "They're highly trained guard dogs. And you expect us to believe—"

"Ben, please!" Officer Krulla said sternly as he looked the guard directly in the eye. "Let me conduct this interview—it's my job, after all." He turned back to Alice. "Then how do you explain the sledgehammer we found lying next to you?"

"I don't know!" Alice cried. "I was unconscious! You found the cloth with the chloroform on it—the one that knocked me out. All I know is that the hammer wasn't there before I was knocked out. You've got to believe me—I didn't do *anything!*"

Joe looked back in the direction of Dr. Breckenridge, but he had left. David stood near a door, shaking his head in grief over the destroyed dinosaur exhibit.

Then, suddenly, the door flew open and Dr. Breckenridge burst back into the hall. "This is a disaster!" he shouted.

"Calm yourself, Jonathan," Margaret Bradbury said, rushing over to comfort him. She had just arrived at the museum. "We can rebuild—"

"With what? It's all gone! All of it! Whoever did this also broke into the storerooms and took all the original casts *and* the fossils! I just was there, checking. We've been cleaned out!"

Dr. Breckenridge stormed over in the direction of Ben McIntyre, his eyes flashing.

"This is all your fault, McIntyre! You were supposed to protect my finds!"

"Look, Dr. Breckenridge, I'm sorry about—"

"*Sorry?* Didn't you hear me? The exhibit is shattered, and some of the finest fossils have been pounded down into nothing more than powder! Without the original fossils and casts, I can't even dream of re-creating what was here!"

"It had to be more than one person," Margaret said, coming up behind the scientist. "One person couldn't have smashed the exhibit and physically moved the casts on his own."

Everyone suddenly turned and focused their gaze on Alice Zane.

"Oh, come on, people!" she wailed. "How many times can I say I'm sorry I was stupid? Do you seriously think I sneaked in here with some private army of anti-dinosaur nuts, vandalized and robbed the place, then chloroformed myself or had someone else deliberately knock me out?"

"It would make a great newspaper story, though, wouldn't it?" Ben said accusingly, his face right in hers.

"What?" asked Officer Krulla, his round face blank.

"Think about it, Krulla. Our reporter, here, was hungry for a front-page story. So she decided to set up this whole vandal scene. I'll bet she was behind the telephone threat and the vandalism. She hired a crew to make good on her threat, only they double-crossed her and left her here to take the blame. I'll bet you get a ransom call for those bones within the next forty-eight hours."

Alice stared wide-eyed at him, with her mouth gaping open. "You're out of your mind!"

"And I'm afraid *you're* under arrest, ma'am," Officer Krulla said flatly, taking her by the arm. "If you'll just come along with me . . ."

As Officer Krulla led a protesting Alice away, Joe stood watching with his friends. But he wasn't comfortable at all with what had just happened. To his friends, he muttered, "There's something really wrong here."

"What do you mean, wrong?" David asked angrily. "You heard what Mr. McIntyre and Officer Krulla said!"

"Sure, but there's no sign of a break-in, David. Doors were not forced open. Then the vandals went straight to the power switches and turned off the lights in the computer room. Then they went to the storage rooms, where the original casts and fossils were. They know their way around! And remember what Alice said about the dogs?"

Sam looked at Joe and asked, "What about them?"

"They weren't here. Somehow they got distracted or trapped or something."

Sam frowned and looked at Joe. "You don't think Alice did it, do you?"

Truthfully, Joe wasn't sure exactly what he thought. He said, "I don't know. None of this is adding up right. We don't have all the facts." Joe stopped talking as Maddy Kingston came over to them.

She seemed to be almost in shock. In a soft voice, she asked, "Have you kids seen Ben's dogs? He's looking all over the place for the Marx brothers, and his temper is short enough as it is."

The kids shook their heads.

Joe looked around and noticed for the first time that the Dobermans weren't the only missing dogs. "I haven't seen them since just after Mr. McIntyre kicked down the storeroom door and let them out," Joe said. "But, speaking of dogs—has anyone seen Wishbone?"

Wishbone trotted through the night, barely able to keep his jaws wrapped around the awkward burden in his mouth. *"Ikkkkh!* Thish sure doeshn't tashte like a bone! It tashtes jusht like a wock! But itsh bone-shaped, sho I shay it'sh fair game for a dog!"

Around him slinked Harpo, Groucho, Chico, and Zeppo, each with their own loads.

Ahh! thought Wishbone, as they reached a certain flowerbed. *The perfect spot!*

He dropped his bone—if that chunk of rock could be called bone—and started to dig. "That's right, gang! See, I told you it was fun! We have to keep these safe, at least until tomorrow. Someone smashed the others! Let's hurry and hide these. Then we'll go get some more! It's our duty as dogs!"

Yes, they had a duty to defend those bones.

Chapter Ten

The next morning, Sunday, Joe sat at his kitchen table drinking a glass of milk and reading *The Oakdale Chronicle*. Wishbone lay under the chair, his head resting on his forepaws.

Ellen Talbot bustled around the room, preparing pancakes. "Well," she said, "I think it's just terrible. All those years, all that work—just destroyed. No wonder Dr. Breckenridge was so upset."

"I know, Mom," Joe said absently, his eyes focused on the paper. The headline was tall and black and screamed off the page:

**PRICELESS DINOSAUR EXHIBITION DESTROYED—
POLICE APPREHEND ZENITH CITY REPORTER**

Underneath was a three-column-wide photo of the shattered dinosaur skeletons spilling off their platform. Below that Joe saw a small publicity picture of Dr. Breckenridge, and another one of Alice Zane being released on bail that had been paid by her newspaper.

Ellen said from the stove, "Wanda's very upset. She

says reporters should stick together, even if they work for different papers. She even helped Alice Zane get readmitted to the dinosaur exhibit. Now Wanda feels responsible for what happened."

"They don't know for sure that Miss Zane is the vandal, Mom," Joe said over the top of the paper. "It says right here that she wasn't kept in jail. She was questioned at the museum and the police station, but she wouldn't tell them who gave her the lead about the possible break-in. The police could have charged her with trespassing, but the college didn't press charges. So the judge let Miss Zane go, but the police asked her not to leave the area."

Ellen poured pancake batter onto a griddle and said, "She shouldn't have sneaked into the museum after it was closed. That looks bad for her. And I know that Wanda will be upset that Alice was trespassing. After all, Wanda was the one who put in a good word for Alice."

Joe put the paper down. "The story says that Dr. Breckenridge is threatening to sue both the Natural History Museum and Oakdale College for failing to provide enough security for his discoveries."

Ellen came over to pick up the first section of the paper. As she went back to the stove, she looked at the front page and said, "This whole incident is very puzzling. It's too bad Dr. Breckenridge is threatening to sue. It looks like the museum did its best." She put a plate of pancakes in front of Joe.

"Thanks, Mom."

"Don't give any to Wishbone." Wishbone sat up with a bark. Ellen waved a spoon at him and laughed. "Don't you give me the Big Puppy Eyes, Wishbone. You always get butter and syrup all over your muzzle, and then you wipe yourself off on the furniture. Don't worry, I'll save a few without syrup for you."

Wishbone settled back under the chair with what looked like a heavy sigh.

"Sam and I are going over to David's today," Joe said. He folded the rest of the paper and set it aside. "He's taking all of this almost as badly as Dr. Breckenridge is, so Sam and I thought that we'd visit and try to cheer him up a bit."

Ellen affectionately rumpled her son's hair and smiled as he ate. Then she looked out the window and her smile faded. "Oh, dear, here comes Wanda. She probably wants to talk about this whole mess at the museum. I do wish she wouldn't take things so hard."

"Yoo-hoo!" Wanda called outside the door. "Ellen, I need to talk to you!"

"I just knew it," Ellen said softly, as she went to open the door. "Why, hello, Wanda. Come right in!"

Wanda Gilmore bustled in, one hand holding her hat on her head, the other clutching several copies of the *Chronicle* to her side. "I hate to bother you so early in the morning, and on a Sunday, Ellen, but I am just so upset about this . . . !"

"I was just telling Joe that you would be," Ellen said. She steered her friend over to one of the kitchen chairs. "And you really mustn't blame yourself, Wanda. The damage isn't your fault."

Wanda stared at her. "Of course it isn't my fault! How in the world could it possibly be *my* fault?"

"That's the right attitude!" Ellen said with a smile. "We all make mistakes. You just need to put this whole situation behind you."

Wanda sounded completely bewildered when she said, "Ellen, I haven't made any mistakes, and there is nothing behind me except a kitchen door. What on earth are you talking about?"

Joe and his mother looked at each other. "Mom's talking about Miss Zane, Miss Gilmore. Uh . . . what are *you* talking about?"

"Alice Zane?" Wanda sniffed and waved a hand. "She's being used as a scapegoat. The child's as innocent as a snow-covered lamb. *I* am talking about my garden! This time it looks as if a whole *team* of dogs have dug it up! Wishbone must have dug in it all night long! I can't even tell what I've planted there!"

"Oh, dear," Ellen said, shaking her head. "I'm so sorry, Wanda! Joe, why don't you go on over to David's. I'll take care of this."

Joe felt a little guilty about leaving while Wanda was still so upset. "Are you sure, Mom? I mean, Wishbone is my dog—"

"And David is your friend—and he really needs your support right now. As for you, Wishbone . . ." Ellen bent over and stared into the largest set of Big Puppy Eyes in Oakdale. "We need to talk."

David was working at his computer in his bedroom when his mother, Ruth Barnes, said, "Son, you have company." She let Joe and Sam in.

David nodded and mumbled, "Hi, guys. I'm kind of busy here. The museum officials are thinking of shutting down the computer project." He waved to Sam and Joe, but he didn't get up or even turn around. "I'm trying to find out something. Just a minute."

The two friends sat on the edge of his bed and waited for him to say something. Finally, Joe cleared his throat. "Your mom told us all about the project being canceled, David. We're sorry."

"It's tough," Sam agreed. "If we can help—"

David sighed and shook his head. He finally looked over at his two closest friends. "Maddy called about an hour ago. Now that the exhibit is destroyed, the Windom Foundation doesn't want to put any more money into the computer program. We'd hoped that Ms. Bradbury and her staff would let us finish it to go with the remaining dinosaurs. . . . I guess it's just not going to happen."

"But why?" Joe asked.

"You can't have an interactive exhibit if there's nobody there to interact *with* it," David replied almost sharply. "The whole museum is closed down while the police do their investigation. And they don't want any of the programmers or staff there, because we're all under suspicion. The police don't know if one of us is the inside part of the group that stole the fossils and the casts and smashed the exhibit."

"Hold on," Joe said. "You mean that they think *you* might . . ."

David shook his head. He still carried a dull ache of anger inside, and he realized that Joe was upset, too. "It's not just me, Joe. They suspect *everybody. That's* the problem." David put his arms behind his head and leaned back in his chair. "At least it's not going to be a total loss. Maddy's made arrangements for me to get the stuff I was working on. I won't lose my special project credit at school. That's something good, I guess."

"You want us to go over to the museum with you?" Sam asked.

David shook his head. "They won't let us in. Maddy's gotten permission to activate the outside computer lines. Ben McIntyre's there with her to supervise so she can let me download my files. I don't even have to leave this room to do my work."

"So when are you going to do it?" Joe asked.

"I've *been* doing it—even as we speak. It's just taking a long time." David pointed at his computer, where a thick blue line was slowly creeping across the bottom of the screen. He frowned, wondering again what was taking so long, but he said, "They're really big files."

The kids sat and talked about the vandalism and theft while the files downloaded. At first, David was pretty mad at Alice. After a while, though, even he had to admit he didn't think she had committed the crime. But if not her, then who? And what about the missing fossils and casts?

Sam said, "If the vandals just wanted to destroy the exhibit, why didn't they just smash the casts, instead of stealing them?"

"Ben McIntyre has a theory on that," Joe reminded her. "He thinks they destroyed the exhibit to make the stolen casts more valuable. He feels that the museum is going to get a ransom demand any minute now. You know, a threat like 'Give us a ton of money if you ever want to see your skeletons again.'"

"Boy, that's really creepy!" Sam said. "It reminds me of 'Silver Blaze,' the Sherlock Holmes story. Everyone thought that when Silver Blaze, the racehorse, was stolen, the thief would make a ransom demand. It never came, though."

"This whole thing's been real weird from the beginning," David said. Then he looked at his computer monitor and frowned, feeling uneasy again. "Something's wrong, guys. This is taking way too long."

"But you said the files were big," Joe said. He leaned on the back of David's chair to look at the screen. "How long have you been downloading?"

David looked at his clock. "Over an hour. And it's a

fast modem. The files aren't *that* big," David replied. He noticed that the blue line at the base of the screen had finally crept up to the ninety-seven percent mark. "Oh, man, I hope nothing's happened to my data! That's all I need—for the blackout to have messed up the disks, or for that virus to have resurfaced!"

For another eighteen minutes the three friends talked and watched the blue line slowly grow. Finally the computer speaker gave out a musical *ding!*, and the words DOWNLOAD COMPLETE appeared on the screen.

David leaned forward, and his fingers flew over the keyboard. He used the mouse to check the size of a file and whistled in surprise. "Okay, okay, we've got something here—a really *big* something." He started to tap keys rapidly. "I just hope it's not—" David stopped and stared at the screen. Joe and Sam crowded up behind him.

"It's all there, isn't it?" Joe asked.

David just stared at the screen. Three columns of white figures filled a blue screen and ran right off the bottom. "Just barely," David murmured. "This data has taken up almost all the hard drive space my computer has. Most of these aren't my files. Just look at all this stuff!"

"How could you have this much?" Joe asked. "I thought you guys didn't get to finish your work."

David shook his head, puzzling over the file names. "We didn't. If we had, the interactive program would be up and running, and it sure wouldn't be filling up all my hard disk." David's fingers made the keyboard rattle. "Okay, let's just see what this is all about. . . . There's the location program . . . there's the digging program . . . here's a program named RECONST.EXE. What the heck is RECONST.EXE? It isn't one of mine." David picked out the command and sat back in his chair.

The screen flickered. Then a three-dimensional

figure appeared. It was one of Dr. Breckenridge's Mundio-raptors, balanced on the toes of its powerful hind feet. But instead of being in the dull green color of the exhibit pictures, this one glowed a brilliant orange, with bright stripes of yellow banding its body.

"Cool," Sam said, crowding in closer. "When did you guys change the colors?"

"We didn't," David replied, staring in wonder at the reproduction. "We didn't do anything like this. . . . Wow! Look at the detail on those scales! We were going to do that visual effect, but we didn't have time. . . . Whoa!"

The Mundioraptor on the screen suddenly yawned and shook itself, as if it were just waking up. The long, intelligent-looking head turned smoothly and stared out at them. The mouth opened, exposing rows of sharp, curving teeth. The speakers on David's computer vibrated as the raptor roared.

David's finger hit the pause key and the vision froze. "Sound!" he whispered. "We didn't have sound—at least not like that. We just had some sound bites, so it wouldn't be only music that people heard. This isn't my stuff, guys—I mean, some of it is, but not all of it."

Joe was staring intently over his friend's shoulder. "David, can you move that thing into a side view?"

"Huh? Yeah, I think so—at least I could on the other programs." David typed and the dinosaur suddenly appeared in profile.

"Now, can you bring up that skeleton program and place it over the reproduction?"

David nodded and typed again. Suddenly, the orange-and-yellow figure had bones inside it; it was the skeleton from David's program. "Well, there is the skeleton and the reproduction, but I don't know why you'd want— Wait a minute . . ."

"They don't fit," Joe said flatly. "Look, the forearms on the skeleton are shorter than the ones on the reproduction. And the skull isn't quite right, either. We've got two different dinosaurs here."

Wishbone paced back and forth from the kitchen table to the dining room table to the big red chair.

This is a criminal way to be treated! Oh, Ellen, I don't have time to be the Prisoner of Forest Avenue! I tell you, Joe needs me out there!

Wishbone thought back to the conversation he'd had with Joe's mother that morning. *Well, "conversation" might be the wrong word, since Ellen did all the talking—so much fuss over a little digging. . . . Okay, so it was a lot of digging, but it was done for a good cause!*

He jumped up into his favorite chair and started to think, really think. *Gotta come up with a way to get out of here. There's a really exciting mystery going on out there. Smart as my friends are, they can't possibly solve it without me! And Ellen has gone and locked the doggie door! She just does not understand that this is a critical situation. Whatever happened to trust between mom and dog?*

Ellen had decided that the way to keep Wishbone out of trouble for at least a day—and to get across to him the point that digging up Wanda's garden must not be on his list of Things to Do—was to place him under house arrest. So there he was, trapped inside the house, while adventures were going on outside!

It's time to concentrate on the Great Dog Escape. . . . Let's see, Ellen has gone next door to look at Wanda's garden. They'll probably come back here together, and they'll come in by the back door. That smells like an opportunity to me. And if a dog can't trust his own nose, what can he trust?

His tail wagging happily, Wishbone settled down by the kitchen door to wait for his chance to make his Big Escape.

Chapter Eleven

Joe watched impatiently as David picked up the phone. "Who are you calling?" he asked.

"I'm calling Maddy," David told him. He looked into the white-plastic container that held his diskettes. "Hmm—all of these disks are full." Then he turned to Sam and said, "Would you hand me that new box of diskettes? It's beside you, on the shelf."

Sam gave the box to David, and he began to open it.

"I'm going to save this list of files," David said. "Then I'll get the list to Maddy, and she can track the files down on the museum's computers." He fished out another blank diskette, stuck a label on it, and wrote something on the label. He popped the disk into the computer and pressed a key. "Come on, come on," he murmured. "Maddy must be away from her desk. Maybe I should call the number for Security."

Just then Ruth Barnes opened the door and said, "Joe, I think your mother may need you. Your dog seems to have escaped."

"Oh, no!" Joe said. "I'll be back in a minute, guys." He ran downstairs, went out the door, and raced across to his house.

Wanda and Ellen were in hot pursuit of a streaking Jack Russell terrier.

"What happened?" Joe called to his mom, as Wishbone ducked under a rosebush in Wanda's yard.

"He was waiting for us!" Ellen told him. "Wanda and I were looking at her garden, and then we started back into the house. We were talking. The very second I opened the door, Wishbone dashed past us! It was like a scene that came right out of that movie *The Great Escape*! Where is he?"

"Right there! Under that poor rosebush!" Wanda wailed, pointing.

Joe heard Wishbone's determined digging and saw that already the dirt was flying.

"No, Wishbone!" Ellen yelled. "Get him, Joe!"

Joe lay on his stomach and reached under the bush. "You come out of there!" he called.

Wishbone backed out toward him, slowly. Joe reached for him and was surprised at how heavy Wishbone

felt. He pulled the dog out and discovered that Wishbone was clutching something huge, gray, and knobby.

"What's he got there?" Wanda asked.

"It looks like a fossil!" Joe said. He took it from Wishbone. It was a massive vertebra, a backbone as big around as Wishbone's head, and it felt like solid rock. Joe looked under the bush again. "There are more sticking out of the ground. A lot of them!"

"How did fossils get into my garden?" Wanda asked, sounding surprised.

"Wishbone must have buried them," Joe said. "But where did he get them, and when did he have time to bury that many?"

From the street, a boy's voice called out, "He had some help!"

Joe turned around. He blinked in surprise at a grimy, muddy, grinning figure. "Jimmy? Jimmy Kidd? What is going on? How did you get so dirty?"

"By doing the same thing as your dog," Jimmy said. "Digging! Look what I found."

Sam and David had come over from David's house and stood behind Ellen. "What's going on?" David asked.

Jimmy, who was a grimy mess, turned around and took something from behind his back. It was a long, curved, gray shape. "See?" he said, holding it up. "I told you that I found lots of dinosaur bones, but you didn't believe me. This is a tooth from a Tyrannosaurus!"

"It's a rib," Joe said. "A rib from a smaller dinosaur. Let me see it." He took the bone from Jimmy and felt its weight. It was a fossil, all right, solid stone. "This must be one of the bones taken from the museum," Joe said.

Wishbone squirmed away from him and ducked back under the bush. He brought out yet another bone, this one long and blunt at both ends.

"That looks like a leg bone," Sam said.

"Arm bone," Joe corrected. "Or, at least, foreleg bone. That might be from one of the Mundioraptors. So that's why Wishbone was digging here!"

"I found them," Jimmy Kidd said. "I always know where to look for fossils. One time I even found a fossil airplane in my backyard."

"How'd you know to look here, Jimmy?" Joe asked.

Jimmy smiled with pride. "You gotta know just where to look," he said. "You can always find fossils under certain kinds of plants, see, and—"

"Jimmy," Ellen said, her voice kind, "Wanda Gilmore would have found those when she planted the flowers. Tell the truth. How did you know the bones were there—really?"

Jimmy looked at her, then at the others. He looked down at his sneakers. "You won't tell my mom, will you?" he mumbled. "I could get in trouble 'cause I sneaked out of the house."

"Just tell us how you knew the bones were here," Ellen said.

Jimmy pointed at Wishbone. "I was exploring last night," he said. "I was out in my dinosaur costume, 'cause I think there might be real live dinosaurs in Oakdale, and I wanted them to think I was one of them, so they'd—"

"Please, Jimmy," Ellen said gently.

"Him," Jimmy said, still pointing at Wishbone. "He was leading a big pack of wolves. They all had bones in their mouths, and I saw them bury the bones here and other places. So I thought I'd come back today and find them all."

Joe dropped to his knees. He held Wishbone's head and looked into his eyes. "Wishbone," he said, trying hard to make his buddy understand him, "where did you get these bones? Where? Show us, boy! Show us where you found them!"

Looking up, Wishbone understood how important this was to his best friend. "Sure, Joe! Follow me! The bone hunt is on!"

He began to pull away. Joe looked up at Ellen and said, "Mom, call the police and tell them about this. These fossils are probably evidence. I'll get my bike and follow Wishbone. Miss Gilmore, could you follow us in your car and take Sam and David with you?"

Wishbone pulled impatiently. "Come on! I'm just gonna use four legs! Let's go! Let's go now!"

Joe was talking to Jimmy. "You'd better stay here," he said. "Tell the police everything you saw. It's very important. Okay?"

"Okay," Jimmy said.

Wishbone looked at Jimmy's face. "I'll bet he's plotting out a whole new story right now. I'd hate to be Officer Krulla! He won't be able to tell Jimmy's facts from his fiction! Let's *go*, Joe!"

Joe got his bike and climbed on. "Let's go, Wishbone! Show me where the bones came from!"

"Gangway!" Wishbone ran joyfully down the street, heading for the center of town. Behind him Joe pumped along on his bike, and behind him Wanda drove her T-bird.

Wishbone led them through town and finally trotted onto the campus of Oakdale College. It was a still, quiet place on a Sunday. Wishbone ran behind the museum, right up to the big flowerbed he and the Dobermans had successfully dug up. He was panting, but happy. "Here we are, Joe! Bone central! This is the place!"

Joe let his bike fall to the ground as he leaped off. "Look at that!" he said. "You must have dug for hours!"

Wishbone looked proudly at the gaping hole and the piles of dirt around it. "Well, if you enjoy your work, time just flies."

A few minutes later, Joe, Sam, and David were standing by the hole. Joe looked toward the museum. Wanda had gone into the museum to get Ben and Maddy. Then Mr. McIntyre and Dr. Kingston came outside, with the Marx brothers straining at four leashes. Wanda led them over to the hole.

"Right here," she said, pointing. "That's where Wishbone led us."

"You're sure those were fossils from the museum?" Mr. McIntyre asked.

Joe stepped forward. "Yes, sir. They weren't casts, but the real fossils. I could tell."

David nudged him, and Joe looked around. "Down there," David said, pointing to one end of the hole.

Joe looked. He walked over and leaped down, then pulled something from the dirt. "Here's another one," he said. "Wishbone must have missed this one." He held up a heavy rock—several dinosaur teeth, all in one lump.

Wishbone was trotting around the edge of the hole. He looked over at the Dobermans, then gave one short bark. Immediately, all four of the big dogs sat, their eight eyes alert and focused only on Wishbone.

Ben McIntyre jumped into the hole and used his hands to dig in the soft dirt. "Here's another one," he said, pulling out more fossilized bone. "And I think there are more here."

Maddy stood by the hole, shaking her head. "I can't understand it," she said. "Even if Wishbone made several trips, I don't see how he could have moved those heavy bones all by himself."

Joe had been thinking about that, too. He watched as Wishbone paraded back and forth in front of the sitting Dobermans. They watched his every move, and Wishbone looked to Joe like a general reviewing his troops. The Dobermans hung out their tongues and panted happily.

Climbing out of the hole, Joe said, "Maybe Wishbone had some help. He's always been sort of a natural leader."

Maddy looked from the Dobermans to Wishbone. "Maybe so," she said.

Wishbone barked once.

All the Dobermans immediately got to their feet.

Joe thought they were probably waiting for orders.

Chapter Twelve

Joe, Sam, David, and Wishbone got into the museum, even though yellow crime-scene tape had been draped across the entrance. Ben McIntyre and his security team were busy digging in the ruined flowerbed. When Maddy explained that she and the kids had some computer material they needed to look at, Ben let them all in through the lab entrance.

They went to the basement. Joe couldn't help but think how spooky the museum seemed. Their footsteps echoed through the empty hallways. The building had that strange air that deserted buildings get—the feeling that maybe, just maybe, someone was hiding in the shadows.

The computer lab was no better. All the terminals were dark, except for Maddy's. She slipped into her chair, adjusted her glasses, and reached for the mouse. "David, do you have the diskette?"

"Here you are," David said. "There are a lot of files. I highlighted the really weird ones."

Joe watched as Maddy put a diskette in and scanned its contents. "Let's see what we have," she said, leaning close and peering at the screen. "Hmm . . . I don't recognize most of these. Strange, very strange."

Joe could see that Maddy was reading a screen full of commands and numbers. "David didn't know what they were, either," he said. "One of them was an animation of a dinosaur, though."

"Not one of ours," David said. Then he went on to explain the differences in detail and coloring. "That's a huge file, too."

Maddy began to scroll through endless lists of files. At last she stopped and shook her head. "I saw some of your work earlier, David, but now I don't recognize a single one of these."

"I don't, either," David said. He pointed to one line. "This is a file called CONSTRUX.11. What is that?"

Maddy shook her head. She looked through her purse, found her glasses, and put them on, tilting her head back. "We didn't use file names like that. I have no idea. Are you sure this came from the museum?"

David nodded. "There are a whole bunch of files that were password-protected," he said. "I think somehow the power failure fouled up the password encoding. Somehow, these all got attached to my Mundioraptor folder. Anyway, the hidden files are available now." He pulled up a chair. "Could I use the keyboard and mouse for a minute? Here, look at this."

Joe leaned over David's shoulder. David called up a folder entitled FOSSILIFEROUS. Joe squinted as the folder opened to reveal columns of file names.

"Here are some picture files," David said. "Let's see what they look like." He called up a viewing program and clicked onto one of the files.

Joe saw a picture form. It showed a rocky cliff face on a sunny day. At the base of the cliff were three red pennant flags on thin white sticks. "What is that?" Joe wondered aloud.

Maddy said, "Just a landscape. I don't see anything recognizable. Try the next picture, David."

David did, and this time the picture was a close-up of one of the red pennants. Joe saw that it had been placed next to a rock surface that looked as if it had been brushed bare of all soil. In the rock were small shapes, triangular and sharp.

"Fossils!" Joe said, pointing at the shapes. "Look, these are bones, still in the rock. They look like teeth."

"Let's try another one." David clicked on another picture file, and then another and another.

Joe and the others saw that the photos gave a tour of an excavation site. The first set of pictures recorded places where fossils lay at the surface. The next set showed the early stages of excavation, with layers of rock being taken out one at a time to reveal more bones. In each of these pictures, a ruler was included—to show the scale of the bones, Joe realized. Whoever had made the pictures had carefully placed the same yellow ruler in each photo. Something stirred in his memory.

"I'm going back to my house," he told the others. "I'll be right back."

"Why are you going all the way to your house?" Sam asked him.

"I want to get a book," Joe said to her. "It's called *Dinosaur Hunter.*"

"You don't need to go that far," Maddy said, looking over her glasses. "Check the bookcase against the wall. Top shelf, I think."

Joe hurried to the bookcase, Wishbone at his heels. He scanned the spines of the books. Most of them were about computers and computer programs, but he saw one book that he recognized immediately. It was taller than the rest, with a bright green dust jacket. Joe had one just like it in his room at home. He pulled it from the shelf and looked at the front cover. The illustration showed a charging Tyrannosaur and a startled Triceratops. A cloud of leaves flew around the two dinosaurs. Above them were the title and author:

DINOSAUR HUNTER
by Jonathan Breckenridge, Ph.D.

When Joe turned back to David and the others, he could see another picture on the computer monitor. This one, too, showed the skeleton of a dinosaur, still encased in the rock. The skeleton looked almost complete—skull, spine, ribs, small forelegs, larger hind legs, and tail. Only the lower hind legs and feet were missing.

In the lower lefthand corner lay the yellow ruler. It indicated that the dinosaur skeleton was between three and four feet long.

Joe opened the book and thumbed through it.

"Look at this," he said, holding the open book next to the computer screen.

Maddy adjusted her glasses. "What is it, Joe? I see a picture of a dinosaur skull in the book, but it's different from the one on the computer."

"How about this?" Joe said. He tapped the corner of the photo in the book.

Sam caught on first. "A yellow ruler," she said. "Is it the same as the one in the computer photo?"

"Yes," Joe said. "Look. You can see that the six is nearly worn off in both pictures. It's the same one." He closed the book and then showed them the cover. "The pictures on the computer are from Dr. Breckenridge's dinosaur digs."

"None of these is labeled," David said.

"I can tell exactly what they are," Joe said. "That's a Velociraptor skull."

"I thought it was a Mundioraptor," David said. "I've worked with them a lot."

"Hang on," Maddy said. She called up another illustration, then put the two on screen side by side. "The one on the left is a Mundioraptor from Dr. Breckenridge's last dig," she said. "The picture on the right is the one from the computer files."

"That's strange," Joe said. "Look at the snouts. They both have a fracture, and it's exactly the same shape. In fact, except for the back of the head, the Mundioraptor skull is identical to the Velociraptor skull."

Maddy called up more pictures and put them side by side. "These do look identical," she said slowly. "Look. The forelimbs are longer, but they're the same color and texture. And, of course, the Velociraptor doesn't have the thumb."

"There has to be a mistake," David said. "This can't

be the same dinosaur that Dr. Breckenridge dug up. It's too different."

Maddy shook her head. "Very strange."

Joe came to a decision. "I think we need to speak to Alice Zane," he told the others. "I'm not sure what's going on with these pictures—but I'm more and more sure that somebody framed Miss Zane. Somebody waited for her in the museum and made it look as if she had broken all the skeletons. And whoever did that has to be the *real* dinosaur thief."

Alice Zane agreed to come to the campus and talk to Ben McIntyre, Maddy, Joe, Sam, and David. The meeting location bothered Joe.

For one thing, he felt the college wasn't the best place to meet Alice Zane. Ben McIntyre would be there, and the two didn't get along. Maddy had insisted that the campus would be the best place, though.

They all met in one of the museum's conference rooms. Alice Zane walked in late and sat at the end of the table. Behind her a window looked out into the night.

"Lie down, boy," Joe told Wishbone as the rest of the assembled group sat at the table. Wishbone stretched out on the floor at Joe's feet. When Alice didn't say anything, Joe added, "Thanks for talking to us."

"I don't know why I should," snapped Alice. "Mr. McIntyre would love to see me thrown in jail for something I didn't do. I'm afraid I don't like him very much. I only agreed to come over here and talk with you because Dr. Kingston asked me."

McIntyre did not change his serious expression. "I'm doing my job," he said evenly.

"You'd do better to find the person who drugged me," Alice shot back. "That's against the law, too."

"Please," Maddy said. "We need to talk. David has found something very strange, and Joe thinks it might even help you."

Quickly, David explained what had happened.

Then Joe took over. "Miss Zane, someone had a good reason for smashing the exhibit and stealing those bones. Maybe whoever it was needed to have someone to take the blame. Maybe that person wanted you to be the major suspect."

"Ridiculous!" Alice said. "I have no motive. There's no reason why I would want to destroy the exhibit. I'm not a logical suspect at all."

"How did you come to be inside the museum?" McIntyre asked her.

"I don't have to answer any of your questions," she said, frowning.

Joe looked down at Wishbone, who stared back up at him. He tried to think of a way to get through to Alice. Finally, Joe looked up and said, "You're right. You don't have to answer any of our questions."

"If you really didn't do anything," Ben put in, "then by not talking, you may be letting the real guilty person go free. Is that what you want?"

"Of course not," Alice said. She looked away from the group. Then, after a few seconds, she looked back. "All right. I'll tell you, though I don't see how it will help. I always have my laptop computer with me. Two or three times a day, I use my modem to get my e-mail from the newspaper office. On the day of the museum break-in, I got some tips."

"By e-mail?" David asked.

She nodded. "By e-mail. And they were from someone

who was using a blind account. Do you know what that means?" she asked.

David looked at Joe. "It means the person who was receiving the e-mail—that's you—couldn't tell who the person sending it was."

"That's right," Alice said. "All these were from a generic account—'student at Oakdale dot edu.' I later found out that all the public computers on the Oakdale College campus use the same account."

"What did the e-mail messages say?" Joe asked, although he already had a pretty good idea.

Alice shrugged. "The sender claimed to know the person who was trying to destroy the dinosaur exhibit. And whoever it was, the sender said, planned to break into the museum that very night. I knew if I could get the story, it would be a real scoop for my newspaper. So I sneaked into the museum and hid."

"Impossible," Ben said. "My security team would have found you."

"Your security team," Alice said dryly, "is all male. I guessed they wouldn't go into the women's restrooms, and I was right. That's where I hid—in a 'Staff Only' women's restroom in the office wing. I knew that after eight o'clock, the dogs went down to the basement level. That's when I came out of the restroom. I was sneaking a look around when someone grabbed me from behind. Whoever it was clamped a strong-smelling cloth over my face, and I lost consciousness. You know all the rest."

Ben glared at her. "So you were able to get around all my security systems," he said in an angry voice. "Even the dogs."

123

Wishbone had been listening to everything. When he heard Ben's comment, something clicked in his mind. *Even the dogs. Even the— Of course!* he thought. *The Dobermans were upstairs first, then downstairs. And whoever smashed the dinos also turned out the lights. And that means—*

Wishbone looked up anxiously at Joe, who had a thoughtful expression on his face. "Come on, Joe! There's a clue here! A vital one!"

When Joe didn't respond, Wishbone jumped to his feet and whined.

Sam looked down at him and said, "What's wrong with Wishbone?"

Wishbone barked at her. The sound was very loud in the closed-in space of the conference room.

Ben looked down in annoyance. "Joe, keep your dog quiet, please."

Wishbone felt frustrated. "Keep me quiet? Can't you see what's in front of your own nose? Pay attention!" He barked louder, then again, and then again. Ben McIntyre winced at the noise.

"Joe," Maddy said, "can't you make him be quiet? His constant barking is annoying."

"What is it?" Joe asked, bending over Wishbone. "What's wrong, buddy?"

Wishbone barked again.

"Take him outside," Ben McIntyre said.

"Something's bothering him," Sam said. "I know Wishbone. He never barks like this unless he's trying to get someone's attention. He—" She broke off suddenly, and Wishbone saw a light dawn in her eyes.

Wishbone stopped barking. "You've got it, Sam! Tell me you've got it! Did I get the idea across? Speak, Sam!"

Sam blinked. Then her expression turned to one of surprise and understanding.

Wishbone swelled with canine pride. "Finally, mission accomplished!"

Chapter Thirteen

"Ah-ha!" Sam said.

Joe looked at her, puzzled. "What is it?" he asked. "You said 'Ah-ha!'"

"Oh—I didn't mean to," Sam said. "It's just that I caught on. Wishbone's barking made me understand something—something very important."

"What?" David asked.

Sam turned to Joe. "Joe, you've read a lot of Sherlock Holmes stories. It's the 'Silver Blaze' clue."

David blinked at her. "The *what?*"

"Don't you remember?" Sam asked. "It's the best part of the story. Sherlock Holmes and Dr. Watson are investigating the theft of the racehorse Silver Blaze, and the murder of the man who took care of him. They go to the scene of the crime, and Sherlock Holmes examines all the evidence. Even Inspector Gregory, the Scotland Yard man, can't find any clues."

"Yes, I know," Joe said. "I read the story."

David shook his head. "Well, I *haven't* read it. I don't get it, Joe. What's the point?"

Sam shrugged. "Everyone assumes that someone—

126

the thief who stole Silver Blaze—broke in on the night of the crimes. Well, when Sherlock Holmes finishes his investigation, someone asks him if he found any clues about the break-in. Holmes says he's found lots. But he says the most important clue of all has to do with the watchdog that lives on the farm. He tells Dr. Watson and the others that the vital clue is 'the curious incident of the dog in the night-time.' In other words, what the dog did was the key to everything."

David raised his eyebrows. "So? What did the dog do in the night?"

Joe caught on and immediately understood why Sam was so hesitant. "Nothing," he said. "The dog did absolutely nothing."

"Huh?" David asked.

"That's the clue," Sam explained. "The dog didn't do anything at all."

"I don't understand," Maddy complained. "How can *nothing* be a clue?"

Joe said, "Just think about it. Wishbone was barking just now. What's a watchdog supposed to do?"

"Bark," Mr. McIntyre said at once. "To frighten off intruders. That's clear."

"There were watchdogs on duty here," Joe said. "Four of them. Would they have barked at an intruder?"

"They certainly should have," Mr. McIntyre answered. "That's their *job*."

"But the dogs," Joe said, "did nothing in the night. They didn't bark, just the way the dog in the Sherlock Holmes story didn't bark. That means they didn't consider the person who stole the dinosaur bones to be an intruder. That lets Miss Zane off. It was someone they knew— someone who could command them all to go into that room where we found them locked up. Remember? That

127

means the dogs had been trained to obey the person who stole the bones."

Ben McIntyre blinked in surprise. "I see," he said slowly. "There aren't many people who can command those four dogs. Maddy can, but she was in the lab that night when the lights went out. I can, but I was in the security office. Really, the only person left is—"

"Right," Joe said. "And I think I may know how to find him. Mr. McIntyre, I think Groucho, Chico, Harpo, and Zeppo can help us."

Wishbone was excited. "Way to go, guys! I knew you'd figure it out—with a little help from yours truly!" He followed the others as Ben McIntyre led them down a hallway. He opened an outside door, and the four Dobermans came rushing in.

"Watch the little dog!" Mr. McIntyre warned.

Wishbone gave him a look. "*Little?* This *little* dog just cracked your case." Then Wishbone turned to greet the Dobermans. "Hi, Groucho. Good to see you, Harpo. Hello, Chico. Lookin' good, Zeppo."

"Wishbone seems okay," David said. "He's sniffing noses with all of them."

"Come on," Joe said.

They all went into the main exhibit hall, where the ruined display of the Mundioraptors stood draped in green cloth.

Joe went to it and raised the cloth. "Bones!" he said. "We need to find the rest of these bones!"

The Dobermans just milled around. Wishbone heaved a great sigh. "Oh, come on, fellas! *I* know what Joe wants! Listen up, guys!" He barked for attention, and the

Dobermans all looked at him. Wishbone ran over to Joe and took a deep sniff of the bones under the cloth. Then he ran down the museum corridor toward the front door, his nails clicking on the marble floor. "*Woo-cha!* Bone patrol comin' through! Are you with me?"

A second later, he heard the sounds of the Dobermans. They were following his lead.

At the front door, the dogs waited impatiently until Ben McIntyre put his key in the lock. The second he swung the door open, they all rushed out, with Wishbone in the lead.

"Follow me, guys! There's dirty work afoot! And I can sniff just where the dirt is!"

They tore through the night, with the humans running behind them. Wishbone heard a steady sound from up ahead: *ka-chink! ka-chink!* His nose filled with the smell of freshly turned earth. Wishbone squirmed under a hedge and heard the Dobermans leap over. Ahead was a dark figure standing in a waist-deep hole, digging frantically with a spade.

Wishbone skidded to a stop. He barked sharply. "All right, guys! We've got him!"

The Dobermans looked at Wishbone for a second. Then, obediently, they all imitated him and quickly took up positions around the digging figure, who stopped when he realized he was surrounded.

"What—?" he asked.

"Sit!" Wishbone barked twice. The Dobermans sat.

A moment later, a flashlight beam came bobbing over the hedge, and Wishbone heard the voices of Joe and the others. He barked again. "Got it all under control! Once these Dobermans realized I was doing the thinking, it was smooth sailing! Here's your bone burier, Joe!"

Ben McIntyre stepped up behind Wishbone. "Oh, no," he said. "You."

His flashlight shone in the face of the man standing in the hole.

It was Dr. Jonathan Breckenridge.

David felt numb. They were back in the museum conference room. Dr. Breckenridge, his expression gloomy, sat slumped in a chair at one end of a table. In front of him were pieces of the stolen Mundioraptor exhibit—three skulls and six forefeet, with their thumbs. Wishbone sat in a chair at the other end of the table. Between him and Dr. Breckenridge sat the others—Maddy Kingston, Alice Zane, Ben McIntyre, and Sam, David, and Joe.

"*You* did it?" David asked, feeling almost sick. "You destroyed your own exhibit? But why?"

Dr. Breckenridge sighed. "Because it's a fake," he said. "Because I didn't want to be found out."

"But you're a great scientist," David said. He felt an ache in his throat. "You've discovered new species, and you've written books that all the other paleontologists use for reference. You've spoken at universities all over the world—" He broke off, unable to continue.

Looking away, Dr. Breckenridge said, "I'm not a great scientist, David."

"Tell us about it," Ben McIntyre said. His harsh voice sounded more gentle than it usually did, at least to David. That softness surprised him. David would have thought McIntyre would have been furious.

"I faked the fossils," Dr. Breckenridge explained. He frowned. "You see, I know that something like them must have existed. They had to. Dinosaurs were around for two

hundred million years. I know in my heart that they must have developed at least one advanced species in all that time. They *must* have. In fact, when I was advising the game company about Bonedig, I used a computer to suggest what one would look like."

"You think this is a *game?*" David asked, his tone bitter. "I worked hard, and you think it's all a *game?*"

"No, no," Dr. Breckenridge replied. "You don't understand. I was doing good work, David—important explorations. The Windom Foundation gave me enough money for one year in the beginning. At the end of that year, my funding would have been cut off. Well, I—I lied. I told the foundation that I was making great discoveries— discoveries that would change the way we understand dinosaurs. I . . . I said that I was finding evidence of an intelligent dinosaur, that the foundation would be famous if it supported further digging."

"And you got more funding," Alice Zane said. "The foundation believed you and renewed your funding for four more years."

Dr. Breckenridge covered his eyes and nodded. "First for two years. Then when I said I could find complete specimens of the new dinosaurs, the funding was extended for two more years. By the third year, I knew I'd have to produce something for people to see. So I used the computer to create the new species. I based it on three real Velociraptor skeletons we found. I added a larger skull. I added thumbs. Then I built models of the species from plaster, and I made casts from the models." He took his hands away from his eyes. "Don't you see? It really wasn't that terrible a lie. Something like this species *must* have existed. I'm sure of it."

David looked away from the scientist. "You're just a fraud, a complete fake," he said bitterly.

"Yes," Dr. Breckenridge agreed. "I'm afraid I am. Once I had designed the extra bones on the computer, I modeled them in clay and plaster. Then I cast them just as if they were real bones. The casts were convincing—you saw them—but then the Windom Foundation insisted on a public display. That meant other scientists would visit. That meant they'd want to see the original fossils. And they just didn't exist. You see, by this time I had taken so much money from the Windom Foundation for my expedition that I didn't know what they'd do to me. It started as a little lie, but it grew until I couldn't control it. I tried to make it look as if some crazy person was smashing the bones. I started doing that even before the exhibit arrived in Oakdale. I tried to wipe out my trail by putting a virus in the computers."

"And you smashed the display and stole the bones," Joe said. "You planned to bury a lot of the bones, but then you would risk having them found again. You really just wanted to make sure that the pieces you had faked were gone forever."

Dr. Breckenridge looked at the skulls and forelimbs on the table and nodded. "You're right. Except that I was smuggling the actual fossils out of the museum one at a time, over a period of days."

Ben McIntyre shook his head. "That's what fooled us. It looked as if it had to be the work of several people. We knew that one person didn't have the time to do all that damage *and* steal the bones in such a short period. We didn't realize that the bones had *already* been taken."

Joe said, "What happened after that?"

The scientist sighed. "After your dog and the others found them and moved them, I didn't know what to do. This afternoon, the police brought everything back— everything I wanted to hide. I thought maybe I could hide these, claim that they weren't among the recovered bones. But I got caught." He stood up and came around the table. He put his hand on David's shoulder.

David pulled away.

Dr. Breckenridge bowed his head. "I understand how you feel, David. But listen to me, please. We live in darkness. The world seems huge, frightening, and confusing. But science can be a bright flame, driving back the darkness of ignorance. The more it illuminates, the more there is to learn.

"Science is pure and noble, David. But scientists are only human. They can be as weak as anyone else. I'm sorry for what I did, and I'll pay for it. Still, I don't want you to think I betrayed everything I stood for. I was foolish, but I did make some worthwhile discoveries. I carried the flame for at least a few steps." He held out his hand. "David, please forgive me. That would mean more to me than I can tell you."

David looked at Dr. Breckenridge. The scientist's expression was pained, his eyes narrowed, his face sagging with weariness and regret. He held out an outstretched hand. David understood. He shook hands with Dr. Breckenridge.

Dr. Breckenridge smiled. "Thank you, David." Then he turned to Ben McIntyre. "You'd better take me into custody," he said, "until you call the police, or until you decide what to do with me."

Mr. McIntyre got up. "Come to my office with me," he said. "We'll make some calls."

The two men were in the doorway when David spoke up. He said softly, "Dr. Breckenridge? I think you *are* a great scientist. You really are."

Chapter Fourteen

Joe looked up. "There's Miss Gilmore!" he said. It was Monday afternoon. Joe, Sam, David, and Wishbone had waited in front of the museum to hear about what was going to happen to Dr. Breckenridge. They rushed over to Wanda, who looked as if she had some news.

"Did they arrest him?" David asked. "Last night he thought the police were going to throw him in jail."

"No, no," Wanda said, patting David on the shoulder. "Dr. Breckenridge isn't going to be arrested. Ms. Bradbury from the Windom Foundation talked everything over with her superiors. After all, as she pointed out, from the recovered fossils they'll be able to re-create the exhibit. And those new dinosaurs may not exist, but the three skeletons are great examples of Velo—Veli— How do you say it, Joe?"

"Velociraptors," Joe replied with a grin.

"Right. Those," Wanda said. "So it all ended up like this: Dr. Breckenridge admits he's been working very hard—too hard. He's agreed to take a six-month leave of absence from his work. He's apologized to the foundation, Miss Zane, and the college. When he writes his next book, he'll explain how the hoax came about. He admits full responsibility and will pay for all damages."

"And Alice Zane isn't going to press charges or anything?" Sam asked.

Wanda said, "Ah, that's the interesting part. They made a deal. She's agreed not to press charges—*if* Dr. Breckenridge lets her co-write his next book with him. She's quite a fan of his, too, it seems, and she's always wanted to write a book! It would be a natural extension of what she does as a writer and reporter for her newspaper."

"Dr. Breckenridge found some great fossils," David said. "And they're all genuine."

"Exactly," Wanda replied with a nod. "He found some wonderful specimens. And that's what the foundation and the college are going to stress. The dinosaur exhibit will go on as planned. And, David, Dr. Breckenridge insisted that your interactive computer program be completed. Your name will go on the credits, and you'll be recognized for all your skillful work."

David grinned. "He's a good person," he said. "I'm glad he admits he committed a crime and was wrong. But now I understand what drove him to fake the fossils. It wasn't right, but I understand. I guess I was wrong about him, too."

"Nobody's right all the time," Joe said with a smile. "Unless it's Sherlock Holmes."

"Or Jimmy Kidd," Sam said, returning Joe's smile. "Can you imagine what he's going to be saying now? After all, he was the one who trailed Wishbone and the Dobermans when they found the bones and re-buried them.

The way Jimmy will tell the story, he's going to come across as the hero of the day."

"Maybe he is," Joe said. "You know what they say: 'Every dog has his day.' Right, Wishbone?"

Wishbone looked up, startled. "Huh? Excuse me, did you say something, Joe?"

David, Sam, and Wanda laughed at his puzzled expression. "I think that you caught him by surprise for a change, Joe," Wanda said. "I wonder what Wishbone was thinking about."

Wishbone sniffed. "Well, if you must know, Wanda, I was planning to stage an exhibit of all the bones in *my* collection. I'm sure that all the dogs in the neighborhood would be thrilled to see such a fine display. The only problem is where to put it. But I've solved that. Wanda, I'm going to create the Wishbone Museum of Marvelous Bones right in your gar——"

Wanda was talking to Joe again. She wasn't paying attention.

With a sigh, Wishbone thought, *Nobody listens to the dog.* Then he brightened up. *Oh, well—this way it will be a surprise! And everyone loves surprises! Wait until Wanda sees how I'm going to liven up all those flowerbeds and rosebushes with my bones. She is going to be thrilled! THRILLED!*

Planning his surprise, Wishbone trotted after Joe as they headed for home—and Wanda's garden.

About Brad Strickland

Brad Strickland is the author and co-author of thirty books and many, many short stories. He has written two Adventures of Wishbone books—*Be a Wolf!* and *Salty Dog*. With Thomas Fuller, Brad has co-authored three WISHBONE Mysteries books—*The Treasure of Skeleton Reef*, *Riddle of the Wayward Books*, and *Drive-In of Doom*.

Like Joe in *The Disappearing Dinosaurs*, Brad has always been fascinated by dinosaurs. When he was a youngster, he read every book in his local library's children's section on dinosaurs and ancient animals. Then he got special permission to check out dinosaur books from the adults' collection. He especially liked the books by Roy Chapman Andrews, an American paleontologist who led many dinosaur-hunting expeditions.

Brad also could be found in the audience of every dinosaur movie that came to his local theater. His favorites were *The Lost World* (the old movie, based on Arthur Conan Doyle's novel by the same title), *The Land Unknown*, and *One Million B.C.*

He also had a very small collection of fossils—no Velociraptors, but some trilobites, some crinoids, and a fish or two. With that kind of interest in the subject, Brad found co-writing *The Disappearing Dinosaurs* to be fun and exciting.

Brad and his wife, Barbara, have two children, Jonathan and Amy. In everyday life, Brad is an English teacher at Gainesville College, in Gainesville, Georgia. He and Barbara have lots of pets, including dogs, cats, and even ferrets—but, alas, no dinosaurs.

About Thomas E. Fuller

Thomas E. Fuller has written four WISHBONE Mysteries with his literary partner, Brad Strickland. But this is the first book they've ever created with extinct co-stars. However, the prospect of teaming up everyone's favorite Jack Russell terrier with dinosaurs—even skeletal ones—was too good to pass up.

Currently, Thomas and Brad are hard at work on their next WISHBONE Mysteries book, *Disoriented Express*. After they complete that assignment, they will take a break from writing original stories. They will adapt H. Rider Haggard's famous adventure story, *King Solomon's Mines*, as a new book in The Adventures of Wishbone series.

Thomas is best known as the head writer of the Atlanta Radio Theatre Company (ARTC), which just published his audio drama for adults, *The Brides of Dracula*. His adaptation of H. G. Wells's *The Island of Dr. Moreau* was honored with the Silver Mark Tyme Award for Best Science Fiction Audio of 1996. He is also writing a series of original children's plays for the theatrical group Onstage Atlanta.

When Thomas isn't writing, he works at a Barnes & Noble bookstore, teaches creative writing, and acts with ARTC. He and his artist wife, Berta, have four children— Edward, Anthony, John, and Christina. Despite the efforts of El Niño and several tornadoes, the Fuller family still all share a cluttered blue house in Duluth, Georgia. In it are a large collection of books and audio tapes, stacks of manuscripts, paintings, all the children in the neighborhood, and one of their cats, The General. This gigantic twenty-pound orange cat wonders when Captain Ahab, from *The Treasure of Skeleton Reef*, is going to come back as a character in another book. The Fullers' other two cats, Mama Cat and Pussy, have expressed no interest in literature whatsoever.

Coming Soon!

WISHBONE™ Mysteries

LIGHTS! CAMERA! ACTION DOG!

FEED THE

By Nancy Butcher

Now Playing on Your VCR...

Two exciting **Wishbone**® stories on video!

Ready for an adventure? Then leap right in with **Wishbone**™ as he takes you on a thrilling journey through two great action-packed stories. First, there are haunted houses, buried treasure, and mysterious graves in two back-to-back episodes of *A Tail in Twain*, starring **Wishbone** as Tom Sawyer. Then, no one is more powerful than Hercules...or rather **Wishbone**, in *Hercules Unleashed*, featuring exciting new footage! It's more fun than a flea dip! It's **Wishbone** on home video.

Available wherever videos are sold.

WHAT HAS FOUR LEGS, A HEALTHY COAT, AND A GREAT DEAL ON MEMBERSHIP?

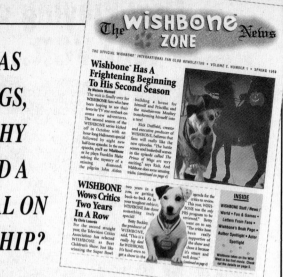

IT'S THE **WISHBONE ZONE**™
THE OFFICIAL **WISHBONE**™ FAN CLUB!

When you enter the **WISHBONE ZONE,** you get:
- Color poster of **Wishbone**™
- **Wishbone** newsletter filled with photos, news, and games
- Autographed photo of **Wishbone** and his friends
- **Wishbone** sunglasses, and more!

To join the fan club, pay $10 and charge your **WISHBONE ZONE** membership to VISA, MasterCard, or Discover. Call:

1-800-888-WISH

Or send us your name, address, phone number, birth date, and a check for $10 payable to Big Feats! (TX residents add $.83 sales tax/IN residents add $.50 sales tax). Write to:

WISHBONE ZONE
P.O. Box 9523
Allen, TX 75013-9523

Prices and offer are subject to change. Place your order now!